Spring Drive

A North Country Tale

Also by Chuck Guilford

Beginning College Writing
Nonfiction; Little, Brown and Company

What Counts
Poetry; Limberlost Press

Paradigm Online Writing Assistant
Nonfiction; WordCurrent Press

Photography Credits:

Cover Photo: Stephen Grant

Landing and Scaling Logs, Aroostook Woods, Maine;
Keystone glass lantern slide; author's collection

The McDonald Boys, Menominee, Michigan, 1881;
viewsofthepast.com; Superior View, 156 W. Washington St.,
Marquette. MI 49855

SPRING DRIVE

A North Country Tale

Chuck Guilford (signature)

by

Chuck Guilford

WordCurrent Press

First WordCurrent Edition, February 2009

Copyright © 2009 by Chuck Guilford

All rights reserved.
Published in the United States
by WordCurrent Press.

www.wordcurrent.com

ISBN: 0-6152-6846-3
Library of Congress Control Number (LCCN): 2008911757

Book Design: Stephen Grant
Printed in U.S.A.

I'd rear a laurel-covered monument,
High, high above the rest—To all cut off before their time,
Possess'd by some strange spirit of fire,
Quench'd by an early death.

Walt Whitman

Foreword

The ancient white pine forest of Michigan's Upper Peninsula was logged in the late nineteenth century by men like Frank McDonald and John "Ian" McDougal, whose stories follow. These two, like many others, came to northern Michigan from Canada. They came partly for adventure and partly for jobs.

In those days before chainsaws, diesel trucks, and helicopters, a season in the north woods meant working half a year at an isolated logging camp, often at thirty or forty below zero. Rising before dawn, the men fueled up with salt pork and sourdough flapjacks drenched in gravy or syrup. Then, armed with crosscut saws and cant hooks, the loggers were hauled by sleigh to the ever-receding woods to begin another day of felling trees. Once cut and bucked into logs, the timber was loaded on horse-drawn sleighs and hauled by icy skidway to a frozen riverbank, where the logs were scaled and stamped on the end with the company's mark, then stacked and arranged like jackstraws in a makeshift dam.

In spring when the skidways went soft and runoff built up behind the dam flooding over the banks, one log, the key log, was pulled and the whole season's payload crashed on downstream. A few select loggers—called river hogs, river rats, or river drivers—earned extra pay by guiding the timber down-river using pike poles and peaveys, wading waist deep among ice chunks and logs when occasion required, to free up a snag or break loose a jam. At a mill town like Menominee, where the river emptied into Lake Michigan, the raw logs arrived in a booming ground. There they were sorted, scaled again, and cut into lumber, then shipped south to Chicago by schooner or wood-burning barge.

Despite Menominee's frontier remoteness, the town didn't exist in complete isolation. Not only was it economically linked by ship and rail to Chicago, which provided executive management and capital for many of its timbering operations and consumed most of its lumber, it was also linked to other north woods communities in a thriving backdoor economy. Miners and drummers, hustlers and hucksters, prostitutes and preachers made their way from town to town along a tenuous network of logging trails and dirt roads that linked places like Escanaba and Ontonagon in Michigan with Hurley and Florence in Wisconsin. Many who traveled this circuit were rootless vagabonds—fugitives or fortune seekers—frequently colorful and frequently dangerous. Operating out of Florence, Old Man Mudge and his daughter Mina ran a chain of brothels. Mudge, a one time preacher, was a cultured man who dressed well and liked to entertain guests by singing and playing the violin. Though guests were entertained in high style, Mudge's operation was also reputed to have a makeshift dungeon containing a chamber of horrors where he disciplined the girls who worked for him. The girls themselves would typically stay in one location for a short period and then, as they started to seem tired and predictable, they would be rotated along, like Burma and Lily, to another town where they would look fresher and more appealing.

During spring drive, Menominee ran over like the river. Loggers just in from the woods filled boarding houses, saloons, and brothels to overflowing. If life in the winter forest was rugged, during spring drive, so was life in town—for men and women alike. Men from different camps or ethnic groups challenged each other in street fights and barroom brawls. Tin-horn gamblers came up from Chicago to fleece the hicks. At a place like Fanny's, a man might blow a whole season's pay on whiskey and women in just a few days, or down at the Montreal House lose anything left at poker or craps. Back outside, he might lose his life. Townsfolk, braced for the onslaught, found their way of life disrupted, their streets unsafe, their tempers short.

The principal events recounted here took place in Menominee, Michigan, in 1881. Of several nonfiction accounts, the most gripping can be found in Richard Dorson's, *Bloodstoppers and Bearwalkers*, published by Harvard University Press. Theodore J. Karamanski's *Deep Woods Frontier: A History of Logging in Northern Michigan* from Wayne State University Press also contains an account and is an excellent source of information on the white pine logging era. In addition, the Menominee Library has a collection of materials relating to the incident.

A photograph of the two "McDonald boys" also exists. According to Dorson, "George Premo has seen the picture. He is a tough man, but he says the picture is more than the human stomach can stand."* Indeed, that picture is not easy to look at, but be that as it may, it is offered as "ocular proof" that the central events recorded here did happen.

Although this story has roots in historical fact, it has long since passed into legend. As Dorson says, "Echoes of the tale float around Michigan and her neighbor states, and can be heard in saloons and boarding houses when lumberjacks and lakesmen talk about knife-killings and witch-healings. No two granddads tell quite the same story, for this is strictly a family tradition, never frozen in print, and unceasingly distorted with the vagaries that grow from hearsay and surmise."*

In this telling of the McDonald boys' tale, the factual truth of news reporting often yields to the speculative "what ifs" of fiction: names, dates, and locations have been changed, characters and incidents invented. But the essential story is based on an actual historical incident and is accurate in its most salient particulars. Accounts of lumberjacks have always been the stuff of legend—their truth, the truth of the human imagination.

* Reprinted by permission of the publisher from BLOODSTOPPERS AND BEARWALKERS: FOLK TRADITIONS OF THE UPPER PENINSULA by Richard M. Dorson; pp. 169, 173, Cambridge, Mass.: Harvard University Press, Copyright © 1952 by the President and Fellows of Harvard College, Copyright © 1980 by Richard M. Dorson.

Landing and scaling logs.

Frank

T HE SKIDWAY WAS SOFT. Sleighs bogged in the mud and slush. It was early April, the end of white pine season. The red-breasted nuthatch and shy snowshoe hare had long ago vanished, followed by the lynx, the wolverine, even most of the foxes. Tomorrow the loggers—the lumberjacks, shanty boys—would leave for town, too. The camp would soon be deserted, left to crows, mice, and chipmunks.

Today the men were restless, waiting for their camp boss, the big Irishman, Con Culhane, to announce who'd drive the logs downstream. For the others, nothing remained but to toss a few belongings in a rucksack, hitch a wagon ride to town, and collect the season's pay.

"Be naught left but skunks 'n bedbugs," Frank muttered, glancing over at his cousin Ian, who sat, knees hunched almost to his face, on a low stump a few feet away. A fine, misty rain hung in the air, but the two wore no coats. A heavy wool shirt, even a damp one, would keep them warm enough.

Frank, the smaller of the pair, didn't mind rain. Wet felt good. When he could sit outside wet and not freeze, it meant spring was near.

"Not even these t'amn lice," he went on, scratching his

scalp with both hands, trying but not expecting to get a reaction from his cousin. "They'll come along for the ride. T'amn bedbugs can stay here an' starve."

Last fall, the camp was just a gap in the trees, a place where sun broke through the white pine canopy to the forest floor when the sky was clear. This camp, CON 1, was owned by Consolidated Lumber, out of Chicago. Such places sprang up throughout Northern Michigan each fall, first in the Lower Peninsula, then when pine ran out there, across Mackinaw in the Upper. Like the rest, CON 1 grew over the winter until nothing remained for miles but shin-high stumps and tangles of slash, land clear-cut in every direction, as far as the eye could see. In summer, branches and needles would dry in the sun. Then—maybe not this year, maybe next, or the year after—would come fire. Splintered limbs and branches would wait out those seasons till a stray spark from some flue or campfire found a nest of needles. Then would come the burn. Not just a few random slash piles, but sky blackened for miles as flames spread in every direction, devouring animals, towns, the moss on the ground—till the earth itself was a sea of flames, pitching and heaving. At last, having consumed even themselves, the flames would flicker and die into smoke heaps and charcoal stumps. That's what happened a few years back in Peshtigo, just across the Wisconsin line. It could happen here, too.

For both men the past winter was a frozen memory of creaking stiffness and sweat and icy silence. But now water stayed water after hitting the ground. It didn't freeze, not in the day anyhow. And days lasted longer. Tomorrow, when the key log was pulled, the river would explode in a blast of water and wood as a whole season's harvest careened downstream.

Frank turned toward his cousin, who sat silently working a bit of wet sawdust between his fingers and thumb.

Frank had stopped trying to figure Ian out, stopped wondering why he kept quiet. Times like this, Frank liked to talk. And Ian, the perfect audience, always listened, or at least sat quietly without telling him to shut up.

Frank was glad his cousin had followed along this year. Except for the previous winter when Frank left Quebec to cut trees in Michigan and Ian stayed behind on the farm to look after his mother, they'd always been together. They'd grown so close, sounded so alike with their Scots-Canadian burrs, most people thought they were brothers.

Soon, whatever Culhane decided about the river trip, they'd head out for Oregon. Ian, Frank knew, would tag along, not to find a life for himself, not even because he was unhappy with what he'd found here in Michigan. Like a child behind a parent, he'd follow, never sure where they were headed or why but trusting Frank to explain—relieved not to have to figure this life out for himself.

Well, maybe Ian *was* just a dummy like they said. Or maybe not. In all their years together Frank had never quite decided one way or the other. By now, he'd stopped trying. Ian was just Ian. That was enough.

"Say aye, y' want t' go!" he blurted suddenly at the top of Ian's lowered head. "I see it in your face. Y' don't fool this river rat."

Ian looked up, his broad face a blank.

3

"Not that y' got a chance in hell, anyhow. It's the seasoned men drives the green wood down. You'll go when it's t'other way 'round."

As their eyes connected, Ian's vacant look gave way to a slow half-smile. He was twenty-two, his face broad and round with a sparse three day's beard on his upper-lip, on his chin, and below his sideburns. His face was strong, muscular, powerfully direct, unclouded by self-doubt and inner turmoil.

"Nay, man," Frank went on. Talking, like rain, felt good, helped relieve tension. "You're still so green I might ride you down."

"Aye," Ian mumbled at the ground, hiding a smile, "y' might hafta."

"Cot'amn!" Frank exploded. "That Culhane. What's he ken? What's he ken what happens out there in t'woods? Hell, he don't see nothin'. Just how often y' kiss his ass. That's all. Hell, it's clear who's goin'—Maki, Seppi, Valin—all them lousy Finns. They got this outfit all tied up. Them 'n the Irish. They don't let our kind in."

Three years older, Frank was smaller than his cousin and darker—in looks and temper. Unlike Ian, who always rolled along at the same even pace, Frank swung between over-confidence and self-doubt, optimistic enthusiasm and blind rage: sometimes a snake coiled to strike, sometimes a clown, sometimes both at once. Other men, especially older ones, kept a distance. Frank was too erratic, too hungry. And he talked too much.

"But who's got more call t'go? You tell me, eh! Who's cut more wood?" He stared into Ian's eyes. "That's right! No one!

Okay! So Culhane don't pick me—eh? So what's that say for this whole t'amn camp? Eh? You tell me!"

Ian shrugged his shoulders.

"It means we're gettin' out a this swamp for good. Goin' someplace new. Someplace where things ain't all twisted backwards like this. It means Oregon. That's what."

Ian reached between his legs for another handful of wet sawdust.

Frank couldn't believe anyone, even Ian, could be so indifferent at a time like this. The two-week bonus they'd earn running the river wouldn't make much difference   enough for a good meal, a bottle of whiskey and maybe a whore.

Still, he wanted to let go in that wild burst of water when the dams first broke, to free up a big wing building into a jam without getting crushed or tangled in ice and logs, then, on a clear, deep stretch to lie back, hands behind his head, while the river pulled him lazily along under small white clouds . . .. But he could live without that. Once the logs reached the big river, the booming company would take charge anyhow, and the best of the trip would be over.

Mostly, it was pride.

Culhane's decision would be a judgment, a verdict. Last year, Frank's first in camp, he hadn't deserved to go on the river, not when so many older men, seasoned men, had earned it. He just wanted to get into town and get paid, blow off some steam and head home with some money left in his pockets. Now *he* would have tales to tell.

Back home, he told Ian how he got hired by the tight-faced superintendent in the black wool coat, the gray silk vest and high starched collar. He chuckled and told how the man's nose hooked a little, like a snapping turtle poking out of its shell, set to take off a finger.

"You go to Camp Number 3," the man had said flatly, looking down at a big gray book where he wrote what Frank supposed was his name. And Frank told how when he arrived Con Culhane, the camp boss made him prove his worth by fighting an Irish teamster.

That was it. He was a lumberjack—or a shanty boy, as he heard himself called in town. First he worked the road crew as a monkey, building skidways for teamsters. His job was to keep up the path to the river, watering it smooth and icy slick from end to end, shoveling horse manure and ashes onto downhill grades to help keep the timber-laden sleighs under control. Not that manure helped much. Though the skidways were mostly level, sleighs had no brakes and could easily rush out of control, manure or no. When that happened, the teamsters just hung on and hoped they were lucky. If not, they were dead pretty quick—no matter how skillful or careful. While they lived, though, teamsters, like top loaders, belonged to the camp's elite.

As a road monkey—"chickadee," the teamsters called him—Frank was the lowest thing in camp, the last served his meals, the butt end of every tired joke.

But he saw who ran the show, how they got there, how they held on. So he volunteered to help top load a bulging sleigh or free up a widow-maker—a cut tree that got hung on another and couldn't fall.

He flashed his dirk, a bone-handled Scottish dagger

passed down by his father, claimed he'd stick it in a man as soon as a tree. He waited for someone to call him on that, but nobody did. By January, he was a sawyer. One of the men.

That was enough for one year. He'd left home a boy and come back a man. Not just a man—a lumberjack, a logger.

During the long summer nights, when his mother and aunt lay in bed, he told Ian about life in camp and about the town of Menominee—about whiskey and cardsharps and women, and all of it out in the open, magnificent brawls, eyes gouged out with thumbs, faces ground bloody by caulked loggers' boots. A dollar a day looked like plenty when you were used to nothing, and when a whole season's pay came at once.

Frank had spent most of that first season's pay in six days on whiskey and women. Sure, the whiskey was watered, the women mostly older and bored, but as long as the money lasted he had plenty of both. And no woman alive looks bad to a logger fresh out of the woods. Ability counts, and those old gals had ability, as Frank could testify in detail.

But that was last year.

This year was different. Frank picked up a twig and poked it in the partly frozen sawdust, poked a little harder till it snapped. Someone else might have eased up and let it spring back, but Frank would feel the limit and press on till it broke. And not just with twigs.

Once, back in February, he had pressed his foreman, Maki. That's when things started going wrong. It was late, about half the men in his shanty were asleep. A few gathered around the big barrel stove, smoking and swapping stories.

Frank lay awake in the blankets and straw of his bunk, the

7

middle one in a tier of three along the back wall. He dreaded the four a.m. wake-up call and just wanted to sleep, but the talk and some bad indigestion from too much supper kept him awake. He was fed up with these tales and the men who told them. He was tired of the beans and the lard and the sweat, but especially the lice crawling over his scalp.

This season the camp felt different. Having proved himself the first year, he took a closer look at the men, and when he did, he saw they were shanty boys after all. The company owned them, it used them, it destroyed them, and it threw them away. If you wanted to get up past sawyer or teamster, you had to sell more than your muscles, your skills, and your time. Frank wasn't sure what that was, but he knew he wouldn't sell it. Not even if he got an offer, which he hadn't.

He looked through the smoke-filled air and the tangle of sweaty clothes hanging like stalactites from the bunkhouse beams. His foreman, Maki, was half lost in an old tale about how he and Culhane got caught in a ground blizzard once when they were out cruising for timber, up near Grand Marais. Half-frozen, half-starved, they were found by a pack of wolves almost as desperate as they. Culhane, pretending to be injured, lured the leader in close and stabbed him in the heart. Then, while the rest crouched at a distance, the two ate the leader's raw flesh and warmed themselves with his flayed-open carcass.

Frank looked up at the bunk above his, where Ian slept. Though the night was well below zero, the shanty was hot. The stench of sweat-soaked wool mingled with pine and pipe smoke like a mask he couldn't wipe off. Lice crawled through his hair. "Travelin' dandruff," the men called them. The bed-bugs were feeding.

Yet the tale went on. Half-frozen and covered with blood, Culhane and Maki, the Irishman and the Finn, arrived in Grand Marais, looking for shelter, trying to explain to a Frenchman.

Unable to escape, Frank lay half-listening, wondering how much the tale had grown over the years, how much the old Finn himself had come to believe. The beans in his stomach struggled against digestion.

"By God," Maki always said to wrap up the story, pausing and shaking his head in disbelief, "those wolves saved our life."

This time, when the line finally came, Frank was ready. He let rip a long, low, cheek-slapping fart. The shanty convulsed in laughter. Even Ian chuckled from the bunk above. Everyone laughed but Maki. He didn't move.

"You laugh?" Maki raged.

The shanty fell silent.

"You laugh?" He crossed slowly and deliberately to Frank's bunk. "You tell me why? You tell me why I don't laugh! You laugh but I don't! You tell me why!" He grabbed Frank's long johns, twisting them up in his fist, thick with soft muscles and fat, his hot, foul breath all over Frank's face. "You say it, by God! You tell me!"

"Aye, old man! I'll say it!" Frank threw Maki's arm back, breaking his grip, getting some breathing room. "We laugh at you!" He spit the words into Maki's face. "We laugh because you lie! You 'n Culhane eatin' wolves! Hah! I ken what you eat, Maki. Beans n' lard, like a' the rest of us. And shit!" Frank tightened his grip on the dirk. "You hear me, Maki? I say you eat shit!"

Maki lunged forward, his face swollen with heat and rage.

The dirk flashed out from beneath Frank's pillow.

Maki drew up short.

"Now you hear me, shanty boy," Maki said, backing slowly away from the knife, his voice firm and deliberate. "You think you take Maki with that dirk?" He stepped up to the bunk again until the dagger point touched his puffed-up chest. "You think so? Then you do it. You do it, by God, or you shut your fool mouth!"

Frank lowered his knife and looked away—but slowly, and only after flashing a look that said somehow wordlessly and in less than a second: "I know what you are, you old fraud, and I know how you beat me."

To stab one of the top dogs in camp would have been plain crazy. The other men griped about Maki behind his back, and Frank had stood up to him, called him down. Now he expected the others to join in, to help oust Maki from power.

But it didn't happen like that. Instead, the men drew away, treated Frank like an outcast.

Even Culhane, the camp boss, who had never paid Frank much mind before, was all over him now: "Something wrong wi' yer back, boy? Ye' can't bend over? Cut them damn trees closer to the ground or I'll have O'Malley teach y' how to bend over! Y' say something? No? Good."

And it kept getting worse. Culhane and Maki had him beat both ways. If he fought back or if he gave in and took it—either way, he lost. They held all the cards.

That's why Culhane's decision on the river drive mattered so much: it would prove what Frank already knew—that the whole damn camp from top to bottom was just a frightened pack of ass-lickers who had marked him because he saw through them beyond their shows of bravado to the deep, secret center of shame at what they'd become—not lumber-jacks, but shanty boys, swamp rats.

And that's why he was going west, to Oregon—to get away from weasels like Culhane and Maki who sold themselves to the company for the right to control stronger, better men by twisting them up inside and breaking their spirits.

And that's why he was glad to have Ian along. Dummy or no, Ian stuck tight. Frank could talk to him when his mind got all tangled. And lately that seemed like always.

Frank looked down at the two broken pieces of twig in his hand. Then he lined them up next to each other and bent both at once, till they snapped between his thumbs.

Ruth

A BANK OF HEAVY CLOUDS hung over the Lake Michigan shoreline, drenching the town with alternate rain and sleet. But despite the weather, Menominee's sawdust main street bustled with horses and wagons. Along the intermittent boardwalk, loggers just in from outlying camps pushed and staggered from one saloon to the next, unaware of the weather.

Two blocks from the town center on Beech Street, Ruth Garrison stood in the parlor window of her new three-story home, looking out at the hostile sky. The mother of two, Ruth was still young—thirty two—and while she had clearly said good-bye to youth, she remained attractive, her beauty sharpened now into formal elegance, like the fine bone China in her dining room hutch—compelling to the eye, but not to the touch. A slender woman, she favored light colors, sky blues, pinks, and delicate watery greens. Her hair was the color of wet sand. This afternoon it fell gracefully along the sides of her head to the back, where she had gathered it into a loose but careful bun, held together by a silver barrette. She had a few worry lines, but high, fine cheekbones and a strong yet delicate chin. Her eyes were like clear winter sky.

The window worked almost like a mirror reflecting her face and the parlor's aloof formality, yet superimposing those images on the wet, gray world outside. The children were still at school. Though her husband, Robert, had often urged her to get help with the cooking and cleaning, she had smiled and declined. Except for her bullfinch, Samson, who perched resigned and quiet in his cage on the far side of the room, she was alone. She studied the sleet that stuck and clung briefly before melting and running down the glass, but her mind was in another place.

She no longer thought much about the future. She thought about the past. Her vision turned inward and back to a solid brick house in Chicago where she had grown up—her father's little princess in a lavender Easter dress. Right now would be jonquil time in Chicago. Right now, jonquils, the ones in her mother's garden, would be coming into bloom. But her mother was gone. So was her father. The house, she understood, had been torn down to make room for a brewery.

She had no brothers or sisters. She was all that remained of those times—her thoughts, her memories—and though she had planted jonquils here in this new place in Northern Michigan, it wasn't the same. They bloomed so late, so long after the anticipation of seeing them faded to weariness and indifference, that they scarcely mattered. When they finally did appear, they were always so much less than she remembered from girlhood, so much less than she needed. Whatever might bloom in this place, she told herself, was too little, too late. And what was most precious, the flowering crab or the apple tree, too often got nipped in the bud by a late spring frost.

She hadn't complained when after two years of marriage Robert had told her they'd be moving from Chicago to Ludington. Although it meant leaving her father and mother, she knew Robert needed field experience before transferring back to the main office in Chicago. Just a year or two, he had promised. But that year or two stretched to seven, and when the transfer finally came, it wasn't back to Chicago at all but further into the Michigan wilderness—to Menominee, this town in the Upper Peninsula, from which there seemed no way out. And what was there to go back to now anyway?

Turning slowly from the window, she walked through the foyer and dining room to the kitchen, where her bread was rising in a cupboard above the stove. She opened the door and pressed the dough with her finger. Sensing that it wasn't quite ready, she re-covered it with the damp dishtowel and glanced around behind her at the dining room clock. Had it really been just twenty minutes since she put the bread up? It felt like hours.

This afternoon, like so many others, was a hole into which she had fallen, surfacing now and then to contact the firm realities of her physical surroundings, before slipping back again into memory and distraction.

Something deep inside her had died recently, and while she couldn't quite articulate, even to herself, what it was, she often felt compelled to visit it, like the grave of a dead child.

She found herself back in the parlor, staring dumbly first at the piano and then at some knitting left on the sofa, but she couldn't bring herself to play or to pick up the yarn.

At least in Ludington, where the children were born, she'd

had other women to talk to, women who knew what it was to be five hundred miles from home with two little ones to care for, surrounded by loggers and Indians. Those friends helped lighten the burden. But now, in Menominee, as the superintendent's wife, she was set apart from the wives of Robert's subordinates. On rare occasions when they got together at a church social or a bazaar, the women acted stiff and uneasy, as though waiting for her to leave so they could relax and talk about what was *really* on their minds—about their babies, about their husbands, about her.

And in Ludington, the children—Mary and little Bobby—though they wore her almost to a frazzle, kept her busy and prevented her mind from straying into the darkness, as it could so easily now that they were in school and she was alone all day.

Robert, too, had been different then—more attentive to her and the children, more hopeful about the future. But the last few years a strange, impenetrable shell had hardened around him. He was absorbed in his business now. She no longer knew him. Though she still felt the strong bond between them, he seldom remembered to kiss her good-bye in the morning when he left for work.

Sitting on the sofa, she absently resumed knitting. Was it her fault? Was it anyone's fault? Could it have been any other way? No, probably not. Certainly it did no good to dwell on it.

Still, there it was. It wouldn't stay buried.

Robert had been a good husband, had tried to be. He'd given her this house, two beautiful children. He didn't like this town any more than she did, but he worked hard without complaining so they could get back to Chicago. Was it his fault his plans had gone wrong? No, of course not. No one had ever worked harder or been more devoted to the company. It couldn't be helped. This was where he was needed. This was the cross that he, that the two of them, had been born to bear.

Had it been she who first pulled the curtain between them? Was it her fault, after all, that they now lived together almost celibate? It was hard to know, harder still to talk, even with Reverend Goodwin, with whom she had sought to unburden herself a number of times. And although she could never bring herself to speak of it, she wondered how much the Reverend had already guessed, how much the whole town had already guessed. The weight was heavy on her and, she knew—although he tried not to show it—on Robert, too. But no words would come. What could she say? And to whom?

Who could she tell about those first few months after Bobby was born? About her emptiness? Her pain? Late into the night, she'd lie awake, listening to Robert's rhythmic breathing, the air close around her as she waited for the baby to awaken, wet and hungry. Then, drifting off at last, she'd feel Robert stir, first his heavy left arm across her shoulder, then his awkward hands fumbling under her nightgown, yanking it up while he pressed himself against the curved outline of her back—panting heavily into her hair, attempting to roll her over, moaning low like a pleading animal.

Could she explain how ugly life felt then? How confused and frightened she was whether she gave in, or no? Until finally, a time came when Robert, unable to satisfy even himself, at last stopped bothering her, which almost hurt worse.

Nor, she thought, was it Robert's fault that he hurt her so badly. He tried to be gentle with her and patient, but he was a hard man without intending it. He didn't know how he hurt her, how painful and frightening it was to give birth, especially the second time, with Bobby. Robert could never appreciate her terror of having to go through childbirth again.

On the surface, their marriage didn't change much, even after he stopped touching her. He still woke before dawn to shave and dress while she hurried down to make breakfast. But now he ate in silence, cutting his spoon into the smooth white of a soft-boiled egg that rested in its white china cup.

"A bit runny today," he might say.

"I don't know what happened," she would apologize. "I timed it."

"It doesn't matter," he'd respond, leaving breakfast half finished and disappearing outside to replenish the biscuit wood for the stove. Then, pulling on his heavy wool coat and winding his muffler around his neck, he'd say good-bye, and leave. She'd watch out the parlor window as he disappeared down the still dark street toward the mill.

And in early afternoon, when the house began to darken again and the corners to fill with heavy shadows, she'd light the oil lamps, start supper, and await his return. Sooner or later, she'd see him walking back up the darkened street. She'd hurry into the kitchen to busy herself with supper, so he wouldn't know she'd been watching. Then she'd hear his hand on the door.

"Mmm! Something smells good," he might say.

"I hope it will be," she'd respond. Then she'd call the children, and the four of them would eat in near silence. After supper, Robert would read or go over some work brought home from the mill while she and Mary cleaned the kitchen. Later, the children in bed, Ruth would sit in the parlor knitting, while Samson sang one last, sad late-night song. Then it was time for bed. Time for another long night.

But afternoons, like today, were the worst—the thinking and waiting, first for the children and then for Robert. She set her knitting aside and walked back to the rain-glazed window.

Still no sign of the children.

She went back to the kitchen to check on her bread.

Garrison

"COME, RO-BEAR," Jacques LaChance coaxed in his heavy accent as Robert swung shut the door to the safe. "We have done with our business. Now we enjoy. No? It is time for a drink." The big Quebekker and his crew had just come in with a solid yield. The first logs floated in the booming grounds, about to be sorted for the mill. The men had been paid with crisp bills that arrived just a week ago by steamer from Chicago.

It was customary for the superintendent to have a drink with each incoming camp boss. They expected it, and while Garrison didn't enjoy it, he couldn't afford to offend this hard-working man upon whom so much of his own livelihood depended. Robert wasn't a woodsman like most independent mill owners. He had come up through the company, not through the woods. He knew the business, and he knew it well; but he neither knew nor wanted to know the details of camp life.

Camp bosses like LaChance controlled the loggers—controlled all of them, from teamsters to sawyers to road monkeys—and with Frank Labadie and his Labor Knights out stirring up trouble lately, it was essential to keep tight with the foremen. Besides, with the crew paid, Robert's work was finished, and it was just two o'clock. Ruth wouldn't expect him for four or five hours yet. On a wet day like this, the sharp bite of whiskey could be a tonic, though he might just toy with his drink until time came to leave.

"We've earned it," he replied flatly.

The Montreal House, where the two now sat at a small round table, stood apart from the other saloons that squatted along Bayshore Street in Frenchtown. While the others were built of rough-cut vertical pine slabs, either fresh or silver-gray according to the place's age, the Montreal House had recently put up a façade of freshly painted white clapboard. Along with the clapboard came a new sign—Parisian red with ornate gold lettering and scrollwork—above the door. And beside the door in plain block letters, was a smaller sign reading "No Caulked Boots."

For years the place had staggered along at the pale of respectability as a combination hotel and bordello. Then Henri Picard bought it. Picard, clear headed enough to see that he had to choose one business or the other, chose to clean the place up. So he set Fanny and her girls up in a new place out of town, kicked out the cardsharps, hired a chef, slapped up the new façade, and raised his prices.

It worked. Picard became an example to the community, and now the Montreal House was one of the few saloons in town where a man could sit and drink without fear of getting his skull busted. The previous season had been so good to Picard that he spent much of the summer in Montreal, where he purchased a multi-tiered glass chandelier, which had just arrived by rail and now hung splendidly above the planked floor and the small round tables, covered with oilcloth— bright red to match the sign.

Picard had created an atmosphere, an ambiance, that allowed the most upright citizens to stop in from time to time without much concern—to admire the chandelier if nothing else. In fact, supporting Picard's efforts could almost be defended as civic duty.

Even so, it was not the sort of place a man took his wife. Robert at first felt uneasy and out of place in his dark business suit and starched collar. By the time the barmaid brought a second Canadian whiskey, however, he'd unwound enough to notice the soft white curve of her arm as she set the glass in front of him. Easy conversation, a relaxed blend of French and English, buzzed around the edges of his consciousness amidst delicate flecks of light from the chandelier and gay sounds of the piano by the stairs.

"This year I bring down so many logs I need *doux* rivers. You be a rich man soon. No?" The words spilled easily from LaChance's lips, but within them Garrison sensed a serious question.

"Not me," he responded firmly. "I work for wages, the same as you. It just means we exceed our projections. That's all."

"*Oui.* But more wood, that bring more money. No?"

"You're right, of course, it should, and in ordinary times it would, but these are bad times. Supply is up, the market is down. Expenses are higher than ever. We have to take whatever we can get. We could cut more wood and still earn less than last year."

21

"Not LaChance," the Quebecker said, tossing down his drink. "Not you either, my friend."

Garrison wasn't sure how to respond. LaChance's voice was friendly enough, but the words could imply a veiled threat. Maybe LaChance had been listening to the Knights. Down near Whitehall some organizers got the loggers to strike for a ten-hour day. The effort had failed, but the pressure was everywhere. A few companies had bent to it, raising wages some places to $1.75 per day. Consolidated was not one of them. The home office made it clear that they would not succumb to intimidation from socialist agitators. Market prices and the interest of shareholders would always determine wages. That fundamental principle could not be violated. Once workers found they could pressure you, there would be no stopping them. Like parasites, they would suck more and more from the company, forcing it to raise prices and cut dividends until it lost its competitive edge and went out of business. And who would feed the workers then? Frank Labadie and The Knights of Labor?

"The company can't give what they don't have," Robert finally responded. "Times are hard."

"*Oui*, but not *so* hard. Argh, enough. Now is the time to enjoy. No?" LaChance's face relaxed in a broad, easy grin. "Come, another drink." He waved his arm to motion the barmaid back.

Garrison watched as she glided, tray in hand, among the tables. She wore a deep red satin dress with black lace trim. Her hair and eyes were dark. Her face was heavily rouged with a small black beauty mark high on her left cheekbone. The low cut dress exposed her breasts, almost to the nipple. Her cheap sexuality aroused in Robert a vague, uneasy contempt, but he couldn't look away.

"*Doux* whiskey." LaChance smiled, holding up two fingers in a gesture that blended with his words and facial expression into a statement at once innocent and provocative.

Smiling in acknowledgment, the waitress looked over at Robert as though expecting something. But he sat stiffly, trying to ignore her. The better part of him wanted to refuse a third drink, to say, "No. No, thank you. I really must be on my way," but the other part was absorbed in the shadowy cleft of her breasts as she leaned a bit lower than necessary, to lift his glass from the table. So he sat in silence, watching her return to the bar for another round.

"You like that one," LaChance observed in a tone somewhere between question and statement, "but she belong to Picard. These girls here, they are just for the look, not for the touch. I know where to go for *that*."

Garrison looked away sharply, embarrassed that he'd been caught staring. He realized now that he'd been studying the waitress off and on ever since he came in. It must have been obvious to everyone, especially LaChance. That's why she had looked at him, expecting him to say something.

Now, as she returned and set Robert's drink down, he was certain she smiled at him, not flirtatiously this time, but condescendingly, almost maternally. He squirmed a little, to think she'd taken his measure so quickly. And yet, at the same time he felt something rising inside that he hadn't felt for too long. Although it felt good, he wasn't sure he wanted that force to re-awaken. LaChance made no effort to hold her at their table, so she wandered back to the bar, where she'd been standing before. As Robert watched her walk away, something in the vicinity of his belt turned over and his shoulders stiffened.

"She is nothing," LaChance observed casually. "You want something good, come along."

"No." Garrison's face flushed. It was out of the question. "I'm a married man. I have a family to think of."

"And so have I," LaChance laughed. "Back home in Quebec, three little ones and a fine young wife, but when a man is away from home, when he is long time without a woman . . .. Well, my friend, LaChance is not a priest. And you, my friend, you are not even a Catholic."

"No," Garrison replied unconvincingly, "and I'm not away from home either."

"Come. Drink up." LaChance grinned. "I know where to go now."

"No. I really must be going. It's getting late."

"Not *so* late." LaChance drained his glass and looked across at Garrison. "The time can always be found. No? It has been a good season. It is time to enjoy. And as you say, 'We've earned it.'" He pushed his chair back and stood, licking his moustache.

Garrison eyed him skeptically for a moment—then, forcing down the rest of his drink with a wince, rose unsteadily to his feet and followed LaChance out the door and into the slow, steady sleet.

Fanny

FANNY DRISCOLL'S FACE WAS HIDDEN behind a thick mask of make-up that gathered in the folds of her jowls and around her neck. At a first glance she looked like a crusted date, wrapped in feathers and silk. Over the years, the demands of her calling had refined her voice to two characteristic ranges— a low-pitched, wet-leather sweetness and a raspy, jay-like scold.

She had worked a while for Old Man Mudge and his daughter, Mina. One time when Fanny complained about her pay, Mudge locked her down in his dungeon for three days, making occasional visits to mete out his peculiar punishments. Shortly after her release, she escaped and made her way to Menominee, where she hooked up with Henri Picard at the Montreal House.

She did her job and he treated her fairly. They got on well for a number of years. And when Picard moved his brothel operation, he offered her the chance to run the ladies' boarding house, he'd opened outside of town. With her previous experience and Picard's guidance, she quickly built a thriving and steady business.

No longer attractive to men, Fanny discovered how to make them need, even respect her. Not so much the loggers, who crashed through her place each spring and fall like rutting moose, but the local clientele, the mill hands, the shop clerks, and furtive husbands—her bread and butter, who needed one spot in the dead cold of winter where some warmth and understanding wouldn't lead to commitments or crank up the gossip mills.

"Blind Fanny," they called her, and hardly a man young or old hadn't wandered out that half-mile from Frenchtown down the narrow, sandy path to the swampy clearing littered with cattails and sumac, where she kept her stable of girls; for whatever Fanny saw or heard or knew about these men, which was often plenty, she kept her mouth shut. For that, and for the services she provided, the men of Menominee treated her well.

Even many wives, though none might admit it, were glad she was there. Her house was a safety valve—something to insinuate about, fight over, threaten with—an inexhaustible mine of stale jokes and clever innuendoes.

No telling how many dull marriages Fanny helped make tolerable. The wives knew *who* she was, and *what* she was, and if the husbands visited sometimes on the sly, well, maybe it kept them from worse trouble. It certainly made them easier to manage around the house.

Right now, with seven girls, Fanny was full up for spring rush. She only kept five in the off-season, but every spring and fall she had new blood brought in from Escanaba. Then when the rush was over, she sent two of the older girls back there or maybe on to Seney, next stop in a circuit of similar places. The latest two rotated in were Lily, a plump auburn-haired girl of about nineteen with green eyes and freckles, and another—

younger, maybe seventeen—dark and secretive. Serious. She called herself Burma.

For a Friday afternoon this time of year, the house was quiet. The real action would start later. Two girls, Lily and June, were upstairs entertaining guests. Four others sat around the dining room table playing euchre. Out in the kitchen, Burma was talking with Billy Kittson, the twenty year old half-breed Fanny had hired on last week as a bouncer. The two of them, Billy and Burma, had developed a rapid friendship, though what Burma saw in him was more than a mystery to Fanny.

To Fanny's mind Billy was as disgusting a thing as ever lived. Besides being insolent and lazy, he was physically repulsive. His black hair tangled and hung chaotically over an acne-pitted face, so that from ten feet or more he looked like a yam under a cheap toupee. Up close, his crooked teeth and the various odors from different parts of his body made him intolerable.

He's showing her that gun again, Fanny thought. *That gun* was the blue-gray .32 caliber revolver Fanny bought a week ago. Billy's one condition for taking the job had been that he get a gun, and while Fanny didn't like firearms, she did need a man around for the next few weeks, just in case of trouble that couldn't be handled by her and the girls, or the dogs she kept penned up out back.

Actually, it was Billy's older brother, George, Fanny wanted to hire, but George was deputy sheriff, and he claimed it wouldn't look right back in town to moonlight at a brothel. Norm Kittson, another brother, also turned her down. That left Billy. No one but a Kittson would have taken the job, and Billy was the only one left. Even he backed away at first, but finally the promise of that Colt revolver won him over.

The deal was struck Thursday when Billy and George came by to check out the two new girls. Next morning when Billy showed up for his first day of work, Fanny hardly recognized him. He wore a dark, tight-fitting suit he'd picked up second-hand somewhere, over a clean white union suit. His black hair was slicked down smooth and parted in the middle. He carried a worn carpetbag. Standing there, stiff and uncomfortable on the front porch, he looked more like an outrageous imitation of a traveling drummer than anything else.

"My, Billy," Fanny said in her low, sweet, wet voice, suppressing a laugh, "aren't you the fine gentleman today."

As he shifted his weight uneasily and scratched his head, Fanny noticed his mud-caked boots. There was no way she could keep the guests from tracking the place up, but at least the help could learn to keep the mud outside.

"Well, take off your boots and come in," she said. Billy looked at his feet, then inside at the worn maroon carpet. "Or go round to the kitchen. That might be better." He might as well get used to coming in that way anyhow, she thought—and to staying there unless he's called. Continuing to smile, she straightened up, filling the doorway so Billy couldn't get by.

"I guess I'll jest go 'round," he finally decided, turning and heading back down the porch steps.

"Don't forget about those boots," Fanny called after him sweetly. He looked back over his shoulder as though confused, then shrugged it off and went on his way. Fanny cut through the house and met him in the kitchen, where he seemed more at ease than on the front porch. He was pulling off his boots.

The big toe on his left foot poked out through a hole in his sock.

"Where's the Colt?" were his first words.

"It's put away somewhere safe. And that's where it'll stay till it's needed. And I hope it won't be needed."

"You don't think I kin handle a gun? Hell, George's got two down t' the jail. We're always shootin' 'em together."

"I know you can handle a gun, Billy. If I didn't, I wouldn't have hired you. But it's me and the girls. We don't like guns. They frighten us. So we put it away, somewhere out of sight, and we'll keep it there, so none of us girls will get scared."

"Well, hell—I gotta know where it is, don't I?!"

"Yes, Billy. I'll show you where it is." Fanny walked over to the pantry, opened the door, moved a sack of flour about a foot to the right, and exposed the revolver, its cold steel dusted with a thin, white film.

"Ain't loaded yet is it?" Billy asked, reaching down casually to pick it up.

"Yes," she replied.

Billy's movements slowed and became more deliberate. He raised the revolver carefully, blew off some of the flour dust, and ran the slender barrel beneath his nose.

"You can't keep it there. That dust'll jam it up. I'll clean it and keep it in my room."

"No. It stays right here in the pantry."

"Hell, that ain't no place for a gun. All that flour and grease all over it. I can keep better care of it in my *own* room."

"It stays *here*, Billy!"

"Well, damn, I gotta clean it don't I? I gotta keep care of it.

I gotta shoot it once in a while—jest to keep my eye, my speed. What the hell am I gonna do with a jammed up gun I never shot before when trouble comes?"

"All right," Fanny relented, "you can take care of it, and once a week you can take it out back for some target practice, but you keep it there in the pantry. You can put a towel over it and keep it away from the flour. Understand?"

"Oh hell," Billy muttered in exasperation, and the issue appeared settled.

That was a week ago. Most of the time since, he'd sat at the kitchen table playing blackjack or cleaning the gun, by himself or maybe with Burma. Sometimes, with a little prodding, Fanny got him out back to split wood or tend the dogs. Last Tuesday, she got him to change clothes and shave. Billy didn't do much, but then he didn't ask for much either—a bed, some food, some whiskey. On the whole, things had worked out well.

A few times, after he'd been into the whiskey, Fanny found him pointing the gun around the kitchen, spinning and whirling and pretending to fire; and once when he heard Harley Sanders and Pikey Johnson shouting out in the parlor, Billy came strutting in like a pirate with the Colt tucked into his belt.

Last Sunday, George came out from town with a gun and the two brothers shot whiskey bottles off tree stumps. Then, when Billy shot up the twelve rounds Fanny'd given him, there was a quarrel about whether he should get more bullets. But those were little things, nothing she couldn't handle.

Fanny was about to go into the kitchen to see what Billy

was up to when the dogs started barking. That meant someone was coming up the path.

"Billy," she yelled, "that woodbin needs filling! And settle those dogs!" and then more softly, "Burma, honey, we've got guests. You better come on out and meet them." She cinched up her kimono and looked out the window to see who it was, but the two figures were bundled against the sleet so she couldn't make out their faces.

"Did Billy have that pistol out again?" Fanny asked as she heard Burma fall in behind her.

"He was just showing me how to clean it," Burma responded.

"Damn him!" Fanny shot back under her breath, still watching the two approaching figures. "Did he put it away?"

"No. It's still there on the table."

The two men were coming up the porch steps now, and Fanny could make out their faces. The taller one with the bright red voyageur's cap was LaChance, the big Frenchman who had been there earlier that day, in the morning, but the other looked like Mr. Garrison, the mill superintendent. What could he be coming out here for on a day like this? Fanny wondered, suddenly nervous. It looked like trouble.

"Burma!" Fanny snapped, "Get back out there and hide that gun! You hear me? Quick!"

Burma

S HE HAD A WAY OF STANDING, hands resting lightly on her hips, shoulders thrown slightly forward so her red and gold kimono hung partly open and almost, but not quite revealed one small breast, both still raw from a manhandling that morning. Now, standing like that near the half-open door, by the small table beneath the mirror where the light-blue basin and pitcher rested, along with a pair of towels, she glanced wordlessly at the man who had chosen her, who had followed her upstairs. Her dark eyes passed quickly over his face and held him for an instant. Then she turned back away toward the mirror, inviting him to examine her.

She had learned not to speak first, but to let the guests, most of whom weren't good with words, make the first fumbling attempts at conversation. It was a little ritual, apparently casual, yet carefully contrived to arouse the man while at the same time getting an edge on him.

Standing like this, in her room's shadowy silence, aware of the sleet's soft padding on the roof and windows, she considered the stiff, well-dressed man who stood in the doorway, his hand still on the latch, looking not at her, but past her toward the bed against the far wall. He remained silent like that for what seemed like several minutes, as though he might turn and leave at any instant. If he did, if he left unsatisfied, Fanny would blame her for losing a trick. He had paid for a half hour, and she knew she had to hold him somehow.

"They call me Burma," she finally said, picking up a clean hand towel and searching out his eyes. Then as he stepped forward, she turned over the half hour timer, and the sand began to fall.

"Yes," he replied without looking, "so I understand."

"Why don't you come in and close the door." It was less a question than an instruction. She ran her fingers along the opening of her kimono and smiled just a little, glancing down and away. At least he looks clean, she thought. At least he's shaven and bathed.

Robert stepped cautiously over the threshold, examining everything in the room but her, finally latching the door behind him. And then he looked at her.

His eyes struck her face like a slap and didn't waver.

Downstairs she hadn't paid him much mind, though she'd guessed from Fanny's fussing he was someone important. Burma's thoughts had been on the revolver she'd just slipped under a rag pile on the kitchen counter. She didn't even realize this was her trick until Fanny caught her eye and nodded toward the stairs. Even then, she thought it was the rough Frenchman wanting her again as he had that morning, but this time LaChance took Mattie, leaving Burma with this other. She thought from his awkwardness and slow, plodding movements that he must be pretty drunk, but she saw now he wasn't nearly drunk enough to finish what he'd started. Well, that was okay. Maybe better. Either way, she got paid. Just so he left with a smile.

"Maybe you'd like a drink of whiskey," she offered. She turned and crossed to the small pine nightstand, which held, besides a kerosene lamp, a half-full bottle of watered whiskey and two clean glasses. She filled one halfway and was turning to hand it to him when he grabbed her by the upper arm and jerked her around.

He said nothing. Yet his eyes again ate into her with an intensity that made her want to scream. But she knew that would be a mistake.

Instead, she lowered her gaze to his midsection and placed the palm of her free hand open and flat against his chest.

"You're strong," she said softly, looking now at his hand on her arm while she moved her own hand lightly up and down his chest. It was harder and more muscular than she'd expected.

Now he loosened his grip slowly and let go.

She offered the whiskey again.

This time he took it and looked at the bed while she poured a short one to settle herself.

"To sunshine," she said, raising the glass and taking a sip, letting it roll around inside her mouth before swallowing. It burned warm and clean all the way down.

He studied her and threw down his drink in a gulp. So, she thought, he's a live one after all. And he's clean. Clean and shaven. A fine gentleman, really. Not like that Frenchman, who kneaded her breasts like bread dough, who didn't even take off his red hat. She was glad she'd turned over the mattress and changed the sheets after he left.

Steady again, almost eager, she set her glass down and stretched a bit, letting her kimono fall open to her thigh.

But he didn't move. He just stood looking into the empty glass.

"How about another?" she offered.

No response.

"I love the sound of rain," she said. "Don't you?"

He said nothing. His fingers were red from squeezing the glass as he'd squeezed her arm a moment ago. A strange one all right. Fanny told her she'd see some this time of year, but Burma thought she meant loggers, and even Fanny had probably never seen one quite like this. Burma guessed he was impotent, but that was nothing. She knew any number of cures. One or another would work on any man. No, there was something more about this one. If his problem was loneliness or even self-pity, she could deal with it, but this was something deeper.

It was as though inside a cold stone wall he'd built around himself, he was burning alive in some private hell that might erupt all over the room.

The lengthening silence made her uneasy. She wanted this to be over. She wanted him gone. But he didn't move.

"Look," she finally said, glancing furtively over at the timer, "maybe you just want to talk. A lot of men do that. You'd be surprised. Maybe you just need to tell someone about it." As she spoke, she reached up to touch his arm. "Maybe you just need . . . "

"Don't you tell me what I need, you slut! You filthy whore!" He recoiled, throwing off her arm, as though even her hand on his coat sleeve was more than he could bear. "You little slut! I don't need you!" He spun wildly and sent his glass crashing like ice against the far wall. "Look at yourself!" He pointed at the mirror, "Look!"

Burma bolted for the door, but he caught her up by the back of the hair and in one long, continuous motion snapped her down backwards onto the floor. For an instant she was aware of nothing but her own screaming and the sound of heavy footsteps crashing up the stairs. Then she looked up to see him standing above her, trembling, pressing his tightly clenched fists into his eyes.

"Oh, you slut!" he half shouted, half sobbed as Fanny burst in. "You filthy little bitch! What am I doing here?"

"Get the hell out of here, mister!" Fanny scolded, waving her arms. "I don't care who you are. Nobody treats my girls like that." Then she was all over him, pushing, kicking his ankles. "Billy! Get up here, dammit! Billy!"

Then it was Garrison's turn again. From where Burma lay on the floor, she watched him push Fanny back a few feet, and while he had room, he wound up and swiped her across the face with the back of his forearm, crashing her into the table beneath the mirror.

"Oh, God!" he screamed, pressing the heels of his hands into his temples as though to hold his skull intact. "Oh, Jesus! No! No! No!" And then he was gone.

"Billy!" Fanny yelled. "Somebody! Goddamit! Billy, where are you? Get the dogs! Get the dogs!"

Burma looked up to see the doorway filled with faces, and as she glanced again at the timer, she realized what felt like an hour had actually been only eight or ten minutes. Now someone, a different man, helped her to her feet. Still wobbly and holding the back of her head, she walked to the window. Through the wet glass, she saw Robert Garrison running across the clearing. At the mouth of the path leading back into town, he slipped and fell briefly. Then he clambered up a slight rise and disappeared into the pines.

She felt a hand on her shoulder and looked around into Billy's acne-scarred face, into his sunken eyes.

"Damn, it's a lousy life," she sobbed, throwing herself hard, face down on the bed.

Billy

I F ANYONE ELSE HAD BEEN CRYING there on the bed, he wouldn't have cared. The other girls all had that look of having seen so much of the bad in life that they no longer saw much at all, not even the faces of the men who rented them, but Burma was different. Maybe she hadn't lost that last bit of hope yet. Her eyes weren't hazy and glazed, but clear and deep. Sometimes they looked into Billy's and made him remember other eyes he'd known or dreamed of long ago, even before he was born. Her hand, reaching up to brush a lock of hair back from her face, was quick and easy. And when he spoke to her—when he talked about the gun or how pretty soon, when Ruprecht was gone and George was sheriff, he'd be deputy—she didn't laugh. She listened.

Now, dirk in hand, he stood by the bed, watching her, hearing her small, muffled sobs; and he wanted to go to her, kiss her and take her away where they could live alone forever, but he knew she'd push him off again as she had a moment before. And worse, he knew he deserved it. He knew he'd let her down.

"All right," Fanny said, "everyone out. Back to your own affairs. Leave me and Burma here to talk a little."

Although Billy let himself be herded to the door with the others, he was last out of the room. He stood atop the staircase, trying to shake off the disgusted look Fanny threw him before shutting the door in his face. Even then, he hung back briefly, wanting to hear what she'd say about him, whether she'd blame him, talk him down to Burma. But all he made out was a low, uncertain female murmur in which neither words nor speakers could be identified, so he headed downstairs slowly, running the incident over in his mind.

He'd been pushing into the kitchen through the back door with an armload of stove wood when he heard a thud and a scream upstairs. It sounded like a fight, and then Fanny was calling so he went for the gun but it wasn't there on the table anymore so he looked under the towel in the pantry and even behind the flour but it wasn't there either and he didn't know what to do and there was another slamming sound and Fanny was screaming even louder so he pulled the dirk from his belt and ran upstairs but a man, it looked like Mr. Garrison, came crashing down the other way and by the time Billy got there it was over. And he knew he'd failed, let them down in his first real test. But it wasn't really his fault. It was Fanny who wouldn't let him carry the gun.

Satisfied he wasn't to blame and eager to prove it, Billy considered what he'd seen. One thing he'd learned during seven years in Menominee was that Mr. Garrison was not a man to visit a whorehouse. Yet there he was, crashing downstairs like a madman after beating up Burma.

Jesus, Billy thought, I shoulda shot the bastard to pieces.

He picked up a worn deck of cards from the kitchen table

and dealt out two hands of blackjack. He had a six with a queen in the hole. The other hand had a seven showing.

It was a pleasant thought—blowing Garrison to pieces, feeling the .32's stiff kick back through his arm and shoulder, the blood surging into his hand, rippling out through his body, as Garrison's arrogant face crumpled in agony.

Billy dealt and hit himself with a nine.

"Damn," he muttered, half aloud.

And what *had* happened to the gun?

He got up from the table and went to look again in the pantry. He was lifting the towel as Fanny entered.

"Where were you when I called? You have to get up there fast. I could've been killed. Burma, too. And you'd . . ."

"Ah, shit! Garrison couldn't kill nobody. Don't even look like he did a good job a roughin' you up. Who took the gun? I left it over on the table, but when I come in it was gone. Ain't in the pantry here either. Just look for yourself."

"You still haven't found it?"

"Somebody took it. It sure as hell ain't here."

"Burma knows. You left it out on the table, and I sent her to put it away. I said to keep it there in the pantry, under a rag, so you can find it. If that's too hard, I'll find someone who can handle it. There's plenty of men around wouldn't mind living out here with me and the girls. Nobody took that gun. You didn't put it away. That's all. Now start looking."

"Ah, shit!" Billy replied. He could go into town and kill Garrison there on the spot, but they'd hang him for sure. No, he thought, sticking his head back in the pantry, there's times you can kill someone and be a hero, but kill that same person

40

five minutes later and they'll hang you like a side of beef. A few minutes ago on the stairs had been one of those chances, but he missed it. He'd stood there, knife in hand, like a fool on the stairs while his moment rushed by.

"It's here on the counter," Billy said, "under this pile of rags." He pulled the pistol out and ran his fingers along the barrel. "No wonder I couldn't find it."

With a long look of pained resignation, Fanny turned and walked out of the kitchen.

"I don't need no help with this thing. Just tell them girls to keep their hands off it!" Billy shouted as the door swung shut. He raised the gun and aimed it at the door. "Bam!" he said quietly, snapping the gun suddenly upward in mock recoil. Easy as that, he thought, plopping down at the table. Nothin' to it really. Just like shootin' cans. Just be ready when the chance comes. That's all. There on the stairs, I let my chance go by. Next time I'll be ready.

He set the gun down and looked at the cards still spread out on the table. He flipped over the other hand's down card. The jack of hearts.

Goodwin

"ROBERT? WHATEVER BRINGS YOU HERE in such a state? Come quickly, dry yourself by the fire while I put on some tea." Reverend Goodwin turned toward the kitchen. Robert Garrison, his most prominent parishioner, had just appeared at his door, wet, muddy, and distraught.

"No." Garrison's voice, though more subdued than usual, retained an edge of command. "I mean I don't . . . .. That is, I'm not thirsty."

"I understand," Goodwin responded, smiling with his warm blue eyes. The pastor was a relaxed, reflective man with brown wavy hair and a deeply lined face, large, yet deceptively quick in his movements.

Without speaking, Goodwin opened his left hand, indicating a small straight-back chair by the open hearth. At the same time, he raised his right arm almost like a wing about to encircle his guest's wet shoulders.

Garrison drew back slightly.

"Come then, at least, sit and warm yourself by the fire." Goodwin lowered his arm. "And don't mind about tracking the floor. This poor house is due for a scrubbing."

Robert crossed the room quickly but gingerly. When he

42

reached the hearth, however, he didn't sit but stood looking silently into the dancing flames.

"What brings you here on this dreary afternoon?" the minister went on. "I can feel that your spirit is troubled. And yet our Lord is a perfect master—as compassionate as He is powerful. Keep your hope and your faith in Him. He cannot fail. Speak now—and you will be heard." For years, he'd watched Robert come and go with his family—so secure and composed on the surface, so needy within.

Garrison finally sat and told his story—as much as he could bring himself to speak of.

"Don't hang your head so, Robert," Goodwin said when the tale was done. "Satan haunts us all from time to time, mocking our virtues, tempting us with sinful desires whose only fruit is pain, endless pain. No, Robert, it is not a sin to be tempted. It is only a sin to yield. For as St. Paul says, 'No temptation has overcome you that is not common to man. God is faithful, and He will not let you be tempted beyond your strength, but with the temptation will also provide the way of escape, that you may be able to endure it.'"

"But the shame, the disgrace. How can I face Ruth? The children?"

"You're not the first among us to be tempted by those elements," Goodwin replied softly. "Nor will you be the last. Our little parish is a ship," his voice began to build, "in a sea of darkness, infinite darkness and sin. And always the waves are lapping at the hull, testing our faith, tempting us with false promises. You, Robert, you have heard the calling of those waves. And you have been tempted.

"But you did not yield, and you were not swept away, and that is good. For there is nothing any ship can set against those seas to match their fury. And every ship must come to port at last or drift and wander aimlessly among winds and shifting tides until it founders on the Rock that is Christ!" He paused to catch his breath. "Cling to that Rock, Robert! If you have sinned, and I don't believe you have, the Lord will forgive you. He is the perfect master. Cling to Him. Cling to the Rock. Go home to Ruth and the children and cling to the Rock."

"Yes," Robert agreed. "It's getting late. Ruth will be waiting supper." And then, for the first time, Garrison looked up and let his eyes meet Goodwin's. "But how can I . . .? What can I tell her?"

"Say you were here with me. That's true enough, isn't it? I see no need to burden her with more. After all, you have not been unfaithful in deed. When the crisis came, you heard the Lord's voice calling you, and the power of the Lord rose up in your heart, and you came to me. Let that be a new beginning. A time will come when you are ready to speak of this with Ruth as you have with me. For now, simply say you have come to me."

Still wet, Garrison walked slowly and heavily toward the door. "Would you come for supper tomorrow?" he asked.

"Of course. An excellent suggestion. That is, provided Ruth is agreeable." Goodwin's face beamed. "Ah, Robert, things are never so bleak as they appear. The Lord is a perfect master. Go home to Ruth now—and go in peace."

"Good-bye," Robert said, backing out. "Good-bye and thank you."

"Praise the Lord," replied Goodwin. "Thank Him for pulling you back from the brink, for bringing you here to me. Pledge your life to His service, Robert, for He is the perfect master. He cannot fail."

Garrison turned and vanished into the lengthening shadows.

The sleet had stopped. A gusty wind tore apart the clouds. From an open patch of twilit sky, the rising moon shone through, bathing the scene in uncertain silver light. Goodwin's chest pounded. He took a long, deep breath of damp air. Then, horselike, he shook his head, stepped back inside, and closed the door.

Burma

ONCE THE COMMOTION DIED DOWN, she focused on rubbing out the pain in her neck and shoulder. In her line of work, rough treatment was a cost of doing business. Intent only on getting what they wanted, their own pleasures, her visitors paid little if any heed to her welfare. But she understood and tried to accept that. It was part of the transaction. She'd had her share of scrapes and bruises and shaken them off, and she'd shake this off, too, and be back to work tomorrow almost like nothing had happened.

For now, though, it hurt in a lot of ways. Not just her scalp and neck, but her back and shoulder, where she'd connected with the floor. So when Lily peeked in, Burma forced a brave smile and welcomed her.

"Looks like you got messed up pretty bad," Lily said. "Did you get some morphine from Fanny? I know she took some."

"Oh, I don't want to start on that stuff. I seen what it does to people. I'll just stick with this liniment. It's not so bad. At least nothing's broken."

"Well, at least let me do it. You can't reach around back there." Lily began rubbing some of menthol-smelling salve into Burma's neck.

Moved by the gesture, Burma felt her eyes welling up.

Lily noticed. "There now," she said. "That's better. You just go ahead and cry if you want. Turn on the waterworks. Just relax and let me work this in or you'll be terrible sore in the morning."

Burma pulled back the warm towel and Lily saw the swelling around her shoulder blades. She began to work the bruised area, gently, but firmly and systematically.

"I don't know," Burma said. "It's not just my shoulder. This whole life is just no good. Sure it's been better here than in Florence. I think Fanny tries—I really do—to run a decent place. The food's a lot better than it was back there. We get clean towels and such. She gives us nice clothes to wear. And even Billy, sure he's a creep, but he has a heart at least. He cares. He really does. The look in his eyes when he saw how I'd been hurt, well . . . ."

"I know. It's not about Fanny or Billy," Lily said. "Or even about that guy that beat you up. It's something we got ourselves locked into. That's right, locked into. We thought it would be fun. Music. Men. Get away from home. Maybe meet someone. But wherever we go its' the same game. In Florence with the miners. Here with the loggers. In Seney with who knows what. Only the deck's reshuffled and the players change." She noticed Burma was starting to tremble beneath her touch. "Hey, I'm sorry," she said. "I didn't mean to make it worse."

"No, you didn't. It's nothing you said. I just think I need to cry a little now. I'm okay really. I'm not hurt bad."

"You sure? You sure you don't need some morphine?"

"No, I don't need morphine, just a little warmth, someone to hold me a minute or two."

Ian

THE NEXT MORNING, SATURDAY, was undecided. Briefly, the sky cleared to a deep, cold Northern blue. Then from the west, a mass of clouds would approach—rolling and shifting, gathering together in ominous banks, dragging irregular shadows across the land. Once or twice thunder sounded off in the distance, but so far no rain.

Ian McDougall bounced lazily along on the last of four horse-drawn supply wagons that clanked and squished down the rutted tote-road toward Menominee. Forearms on his thighs, legs hanging over the wagon's back edge, he watched the muddy road reel out beneath his boots. A few minutes ago he'd been watching the cloud show, but now he let the sun fall on top of his head and across the back of his shoulders. His cousin rode beside him.

He tried to think about Oregon, a place Frank said was different, a place they'd head for in a couple of days, after getting paid. He tried to make a picture of Oregon come into his head, but nothing developed. Frank said it was a better life there, said the winters weren't so hard, the trees were twice as big as these, and the pay was right. But that's how Frank had talked about Michigan last year, and here he was aching to move on, to trek across the country to a place where they had bigger trees and the winters weren't so cold. But it wasn't just that, Frank said, but something else. Out West things were different somehow, so a man could be a man and not get cut down for it.

That was the main thing with Frank, not getting cut down.

Ian wasn't anxious to go west. These trees were tall enough. Winters weren't any colder here than back home. Sure, life got hard sometimes, but it was a good life, too, if you didn't worry about what folks said and just did your job. Ian didn't much trust words. He seldom used them himself and didn't listen much when others did. He knew they called him a dummy, and knew what it meant, but he knew, too, that "dummy" was just a word people stuck on him and not worth all the talking and fighting it would take to shake it off. And he knew the word would follow him to Oregon, just like trouble would follow Frank, no matter what either of them did.

Besides, Michigan was closer to home. First Frank had said they'd go back home come spring, but now he'd changed his mind, and that made it hard because Ian had told his mother and sister he'd be back for seedtime to help put in crops, but if he went with Frank, his mother and sister would just keep waiting and wondering, but he wouldn't ever come back, and they'd never know why, and that didn't seem right.

Still, he didn't want to go home alone. He knew if he did, he'd never get away again. He'd be trapped in that little cabin the rest of his life, and die there just like his pa. No. Better to head west with Frank. He didn't feel good about it, though. It was one of those times he wished he'd learned to write, so he could tell them, at least, that he was all right, that he still loved them, would try to get back to see them.

The thought made his chest tighten, and his face clench. He knew he had to get home again sometime, but he couldn't see how it could happen. It will be hard, he thought. It will be hard.

The wagon lurched and sank with a heavy thud. A whip cracked, and they lunged sharply forward—only to sink back down again.

"Awright boys, git off 'n push!" the teamster shouted back. The men climbed down and looked for the trouble. The left front wheel had got hung in a sink-hole, not deep—only about eight inches—but though the road had been mostly leveled, the wagon was on an uphill grade now, the horses were starting to tire, and the hole had a sharp rock lip on the front that they had to go up and over. Almost reflexively, Ian grabbed the wagon frame above the wheel and began lifting. The other men went around back to push.

"Hee—yah! Yah!" The whip cracked high and loud above the horses. "Move it you bastards! Pull!" The wagon lurched forward again. The men behind leaned into it, groaning. "Hey back there, bear bait! Push! Throw some meat in it, you swampers! Hee-yah!"

The wheel was up on the lip now. They had it. Ian lifted hard, from his boots clear up to the top of his head till the veins in his face and his arms stood out, till he lost consciousness of all but the lifting. And then he felt the weight at last get up there, up over the lip and roll out from under his lifting before he could stop.

He collapsed forward slightly, as the men let out a short cheer and scrambled back aboard. Moving now, the wagon didn't stop. Ian watched it for a second while he caught his breath.

"Come on, Dummy!" someone shouted. "You want to get left behind?!" Trotting a few quick paces, he jumped back aboard in the same spot he sat before.

He felt Frank's displeasure beside him. He knew what Frank would have done. He'd have called down the man who said "Dummy" and made him take it back, but it seemed to Ian that once you started calling people down, it was hard to stop. It only made for trouble and hard feelings, which Ian didn't like, but which Frank seemed to crave like tobacco. Ian waited for Frank to say something. He expected a rebuke. But it didn't come.

Frank just kept quiet, like he had most of the time since he found out for sure he wasn't going down the river. Once or twice he'd started to talk or make a joke, but his words had no force. Had no feeling behind them. In his mind he was somewhere else completely—on the river maybe, or in Oregon. But Ian didn't care about either the river or Oregon. He forgot about Frank again.

He was remembering winter. He would miss that almost as much as his mother and sister. He couldn't imagine cutting wood in warm weather. Sure these Northern winters got hard at times, but something happened to the world at about thirty five or forty below zero. A fine tension crackled in the frozen air. It huddled outside the shanty at night while you slept. And in the day while you worked, it informed every act, an absolute silence that magnified the slightest sound: the crunch of each boot step, each axe chink, skipped clean and true off of one frozen surface then another like a rock across water until swallowed back up into silence.

Or that first slow bite of saw teeth into pine, and the way your blood began to warm and your muscles to loosen as you and your partner built rhythm with the seven foot crosscut, as the blade began to warm and sing in its groove—pull and rip and feel the blade drawn back away, then pull and rip and let the blade slide away again—until the tree lifted up from the blade and your heart lifted into your forehead as you heard the wood begin to crack and shouted, "Timbuur!" Watched the huge pine lean and pick up speed and topple, right where you'd figured, in a rush of wind and needles onto the snow, branches popping like toothpicks. The tree would bounce, almost thrash like a dying animal, on the ground for an instant. And then lie still.

He'd heard Indians, even some whites, say each tree had a spirit, each animal, too, not just humans—and he in part believed it. His heart would pump fast then, his eyes burn like coals.

And on it would go all day, interrupted by a couple of lunches. Pull and rip, pull and rip—until your arms hung so heavy you could hardly lift them, and the sky grew too dark again to see. Then, on a still evening, you might hear the barred owl calling, far off at the border of pure sound and language: *hooo . . . hoo coox . . . hooo cooks fur yooo*. And you climbed atop the last loaded sleigh back to camp and felt the night air take hold of you again, felt the need for food and sleep. And that was all you needed, all you wanted. And you knew you could have them. And they were good.

"Couple hours more till we be there," Frank said. Ian looked over at him and nodded slightly. "We get us some sweet, wet pussy. You ready fer that?" Frank rubbed his hand up and down rhythmically over his crotch.

Ian chuckled to himself. Sure he was ready, but not like Frank. "I kin wait till we get there," he said.

"Sure you kin wait. I guess you kin wait till yer cock falls off. Not me."

The remark held more truth than Frank knew, but Ian didn't much care. Frank, if you could believe him, was a skilled and dedicated cocksman, but Ian was sort of slow getting up and quick on the trigger once in the groove. So far he'd never failed completely, but even so, the pleasures seldom outbalanced the awkwardness and embarrassment. Sometimes he wondered how it would be to make love with a real woman and not just a whore, wondered if it would be any different. Frank claimed they all were whores deep down, but Ian wasn't so sure. And he doubted even Frank fully believed it—just some words he'd heard someone say somewhere and picked up and repeated. He thought of his mother and sister, remembered when he was little, his father home night after night silently smoking his pipe, then disappearing, going off to Montreal, once for almost a year. And he wondered. It was all too knotty and depressing to think about—not like felling timber in the January forest.

As the wagon crested another small hill, Ian looked back down the north side at the shadowy blue-grey landscape—the patches of ice and snow still crusty and firm. Ahead, the downhill grade was deep slush.

"Aye—" Frank went on, "we won't stay there long anyhow. Those maggots'll have all our pockets cleaned out in a couple days if we let 'em. But that ain't gonna happen. First thing we get paid we get us a stake—a wagon, a team, some supplies. Whatever we need. Been thinkin' a bit about that. We'll want stout horses, big Western grays or Canada blacks. Then—what we got left—aye. We can blow it on whiskey or women. Whatever we choose. Okay. But first off, we get up our stake and get ready to go."

Ian looked at his cousin's face. A wagon. A team? Supplies? Oregon? It was hard to understand how these things could be so real to Frank. For Ian, they were only words. Frank was always thinking about tomorrow or the next day. Wherever Frank had been or whatever he had done, nothing today was as good as it would be tomorrow. Frank had big dreams. He knew how to look ahead. Michigan had been good. Oregon might be better. Or maybe it didn't matter. Anyhow, Ian would come along and see.

George

GEORGE KITTSON, BILLY'S OLDER BROTHER, was deputy sheriff. Today he sat in the sheriff's office alone, except for his one prisoner, an old Indian—a Menominee. *People of the wild rice*, the name means; white Indians some folks called them. The old man slept curled like a fetus with his mouth open, dripping saliva and blood-flecked mucus. From time to time, he broke into violent spasms of coughing and retching till his face began to turn purple and his eyes got all bugged out. Then George went over and swung open the unlocked cell door, grabbed him up and shook him like a cherry tree to make him stop.

When this didn't help, which was almost every time, George threw the Indian back down on the cot and cussed him till he started sobbing and moaning some strange, mournful chant which George, though part Menominee himself, couldn't understand. Then George started yelling: "Shut up, y' useless drunk, 'n go back t' sleep! You ain't gonna die yet. You ain't that lucky! Now shut the hell up!" Till pretty soon the Indian rolled over and passed out again.

That's how it had been all day, except for about an hour when Billy came by. Even then, the Indian made such a commotion George could hardly keep his mind on what Billy said—something about Robert Garrison coming out to Fanny's, going berserk and beating up a whore. It sounded crazy, and George couldn't get it straight because of the Indian's wailing. By the time George finally figured out what Billy was saying, he didn't believe it. But now with Billy back out to Fanny's and the Indian silent, he could run it over in his mind.

What if it *was* true?—he wondered. What did that mean for him? Not that it concerned him as a lawman. The law, as Sheriff Ruprecht had explained most clearly, didn't care about whorehouse brawls. Not in Menominee. Unless it was something serious like killing or robbery. Otherwise, when the law came to a brothel, it came as a guest. That was the best way. Ruprecht had said that ever since George became deputy, and George was glad to discover how much those ladies respected the law and how well they could treat it.

So he began thinking this news from Billy could prove useful. He remembered Ruprecht telling him, "It ain't what you *do* that makes you a good sheriff. It's what you *know*—about people. If you *know* enough, you don't have to *do* nothing special to keep them in line." According to the sheriff, when you worked the job long enough, you learned things, and knowing those things gave you choices until finally, if you were really good like Ruprecht, you actually *became* the law—a swift glance, a quiet warning, you hardly ever needed more than that. When you did, you called on your deputy. He was your muscle. George understood that, and he didn't mind being a muscle, but he wanted more. He wanted to be the law.

This Garrison thing, if it was true—and Billy couldn't have made up the whole story—could be useful. So George began trying to figure out how.

Ruprecht

WHILE GEORGE SAT THERE IN THOUGHT with his feet cocked up on the broad desk, the door swung open. It was Ruprecht, a big, bristly looking man with tobacco-stained teeth and silver-flecked red hair. His right eye was blue, but his left one was brown—glass—and sometimes it floated and wandered aimlessly in its socket.

"This what you been doin' all afternoon?" Ruprecht asked, watching George swing his legs down self-consciously and straighten himself in the chair. "This what you get paid for? This how you get to be sheriff when I step down?" Ruprecht had been talking like that for years, about how he was getting too old to wear a badge, how he needed a rest, how he'd step down the minute he saw the man who could replace him. He'd long ago convinced himself George wasn't that man. It was good for a deputy to be mean and stupid, Ruprecht figured—but not for a sheriff.

"Hell! I been looking after that drunken Indian over there, wailin' and coughin' and pukin' his guts all day, while you been out makin' the rounds."

"He keep you awake then?" Ruprecht taunted.

"Damn!" George snapped, jumping up from the desk. "I

58

ain't been sleepin', and you know it!"

"Looks like you beat him up pretty good." Ruprecht motioned with his head toward the Indian, keeping his good eye fixed on George.

"Aw, hell. That ain't much. I just had to shut him up a few times, that's all. Me 'n Billy was tryin' to talk. He kep' . . . "

"Billy been here today?"

"Yeah, why?"

"We don't need no pimps hangin' round here. I told you that. It don't look good."

"You mean my own brother can't come by to tell me some news?

"Not if he's gonna pimp, he can't. You want news about Fanny's place, you go out there 'n get it. We don't need no pimps or whores hanging out round the office."

"Why you son of a . . . "

"You jus' better hope this old chief here wakes up." He nodded back in the direction of the Indian. "Cause if he don't, you got trouble."

"Aw, hell, he's okay. Look how he's twitchin' aroun' over there. He ain't bad."

"You better hope so. You better hope he don't need no doctor. We don't need no doctors 'round here any more'n we need pimps. Now get out there 'n make your rounds—and don't come back drunk."

"Ah, shit!" George spit the words then spun around and out the door.

Ruprecht winced slightly at the slam. Alone suddenly in the quiet room, he realized he, himself, was slightly drunk.

Tired and a little dizzy from his rounds, he sat down behind his desk, laid his head on his arms, and fell asleep.

Garrison

ALTHOUGH IT WAS LATE SATURDAY AFTERNOON by now, Robert hadn't felt right all day. He wasn't hung over. He hadn't had that much to drink the day before, and talking with Reverend Goodwin had somewhat assuaged his guilt for his actions. Wasn't it true, as Goodwin had pointed out, that Robert, in the end, had beaten down temptation and behaved honorably, even struck a blow for the good? Yet for all that, he couldn't shake his humiliation at visiting a brothel in the first place or the painful embarrassment at having to hide it from Ruth, like a wayward schoolboy. Even more, he worried that she'd hear of it somehow and be badly wounded.

The morning had begun more slowly than usual. Robert stayed in bed past eight o'clock, feigning sleep till he heard Ruth below in the kitchen making breakfast. When he went down to eat, he passed quickly over his food, taking only bacon and a few bites of one egg. He spent most of the morning pacing from parlor to dining room, then on to the kitchen, then back, pausing only to look at Samson in his cage, or to bark a command or a warning at the children. Finally, Mary and Bobby put on their coats and went outside.

Alone with Ruth, he saw, though she tried not to show it,

that she was upset. She couldn't know exactly what he'd done, of course, but she'd know it was serious since he'd seen Goodwin. She knew Robert didn't care much for the pastor and wouldn't drop by just to visit. And not only that, but the liquor on his breath and the mud on his clothes.

So when she sat down in the parlor and began polishing the silver, Robert sat also and tried to read the latest *American Lumberman*, but he couldn't concentrate. She was too quiet, and he felt her staring at him, although she wasn't.

She looked up from her work only once—to remark again how thoughtful it was to invite the Reverend to dinner and that she only wondered why he hadn't mentioned his intention beforehand. And when she accepted so easily his explanation that it was an impulse, a spur of the moment decision, Robert knew she understood that Goodwin was somehow involved in whatever had happened. Then she grew even quieter, and although the silver was meticulously clean, she kept polishing anyway, as though she intended to rub away even the memory of the smallest speck of tarnish on the inner tongs of the last fork.

And so, he left at noon for the office with mixed feelings. It was good to get out from under her heavy silence, and yet he felt almost as if he was running away from her. He thought she looked doubtful when he told her he had to go pay off a crew that was coming in. And he resented Culhane's bringing his boys in on Saturday instead of Friday like LaChance, or on Monday. This was Culhane's way of reminding Garrison that out in the camps men worked a six day week every week as a matter of course. No Saturdays off for a logger.

Even so, it did feel good to be out of the house where Ruth's complex anxiety weighed him down so, to be back in this ordered world of dollars and board feet and contracts, beyond reach of preachers or women.

The afternoon passed quickly until around four o'clock when he realized Culhane was about two hours later than promised. True, the roads were bad and the wagons might have started off late; even so, this wasn't like Culhane. He was ambitious and generally reliable. That's why he was camp boss. He said he'd be here, and he would. He didn't make mistakes.

Still, this might be his year to slip. LaChance, after all, was already in, with a million and a half board feet coming down the river. According to the scalers, he'd cut at least a hundred thousand more than Culhane would deliver.

Thinking of LaChance made Garrison uneasy. The Quebecker was too clever, too unpredictable. He pushed too much. And now, yesterday's incident gave him something he could use like a wedge to drive further into the business. LaChance would have a hold on him and wouldn't hesitate to use it. The more Garrison thought about the incident, the clearer that became.

Goodwin, too, would have a hold on him, though he surely wouldn't use it for personal gain. Still, he could if he wanted something badly enough.

And what about Fanny Driscoll? No, she'd keep quiet or Robert would destroy her and her nasty little business. Her position was too precarious to risk even a hint of blackmail. She was no threat, but God how he loathed her, and that uppity little whore, and LaChance, too, for dragging him out there.

Robert got up from his desk and began pacing. Almost five o'clock and still no sign of Culhane. Where the hell was he? Soon Goodwin would be arriving for dinner, and Garrison didn't want him alone with Ruth. He'd seen those two together before, and he sensed some private compact between them, and he knew in a group of three, two often pair up against the third. And so, he wanted to be there from the start to keep the balance in his favor.

And still Culhane hadn't arrived. Garrison couldn't decide whether to continue waiting here at the office or get home and take care of the more urgent matter before Goodwin gave something away.

Ruth had to be told—and soon, no matter how painful for the both of them. That much was clear now. It was the only way he could keep the incident from being turned against him. He had to stop trouble fast, before it got started. He had to get home.

At 5:15 Robert closed the sawmill door, turned up his collar, and stepped into the windy half-dark street. Just as he turned toward home, he heard wagons. The safe was locked. The payroll records, which he had kept out on his desk all day, were back in the filing cabinet where they belonged, and Robert was bracing for the confrontation at home as the Culhane and his crew rolled out of the shadows.

The wagons slogged up Bayshore from Finntown, creaking and grinding, the loggers—raucous, vulgar, filthy—clinging like flies to excrement. Never had these swamp rats angered and revolted him so thoroughly. His eyes searched out Culhane and found him, riding shotgun on the lead wagon.

Frank

A FINE PLACE, FRANK THOUGHT, looking down the long, narrow attic. And compared to the shanty he'd slept in all winter, it was. Twice the shanty's size, the attic held only one bed, set beneath the small semi-circular window at the back, but a real bed, an iron-framed double, with a mattress—not another pine slab topped with evergreen boughs and straw.

"How much?" he asked, rubbing his thumb across his fingers.

"Dollar a night. Six a week," the owner replied. His heavy Finnish accent reminded Frank of Maki. Culhane had stopped the wagons here in Finntown to talk with someone he knew on the street. When Frank saw they'd be awhile, he and Ian jumped off to find a room, thinking to get first pick.

"Okay," Frank said. Hard to know how much English this old Finn understood. "And we be needin' a bath, too." He lifted his left arm and made a kind of washing movement up under the armpit and back across the chest. Most of these Finns understood whatever they wanted—and nothing else. Most had blank, round faces that gave little away. This one was no exception.

"Two bits a bath. Hot," the Finn answered, and Frank's mind was made up.

"Okay, we take it." Frank nodded his head. "We go get our money and gear, eh." He, pointed down toward the Continental Lumber building, where he imagined the others lined up for their pay.

"Mmmmh. Money." The old man rubbed his thumb across his fingers as Frank had a moment earlier.

"Aye, that's where we headin', tammit. To get money," Frank snapped back.

"Mmmmh. Get money!"

Frank shook his head in disgust. "Come on, Ian, let's move, eh. This bastard won't let us the room till he sees our money." Ian sat on the bed looking out the low, half-round window. He didn't move.

Frank continued, "You want that side by the window, that it? It's yours, but we gotta go get paid or you won't have any side, will y'?"

Ian got up and headed for a hole in the far corner of the floor where a steep, unfinished stairway of still green slab wood ran down from the attic to the hallway below. Frank watched his cousin's head vanish through the hole and nodded for the old man to go next. Then he took another look around to impress the attic on his memory, as though that strengthened his claim.

He liked the room almost as much as he disliked its owner. Although filled with late-afternoon shadows, it was airy and clean. Roofing nails poked through the ceiling like tiny stalactites in a cave. The floor had been recently planked with rough cut one by sixes. It smelled like the forest, not like the bunkhouse, which reeked of stale smoke and sweat. Probably

66

the floor like the staircase was the old man's work, Frank thought climbing down to the hallway.

As his head emerged from the attic, he became aware of a sharp, scolding woman's voice, and looked back down over his shoulder to see her, large and squinty-eyed in a faded cotton housedress and lavender apron, her hair pulled back tight in a bun. She held her finger in Ian's astonished face and lectured in Finnish, while he stood looking back up the stairs for Frank, shifting his weight from foot to foot.

Now she saw Frank coming through the hole, and getting no satisfaction from Ian, turned on him. But Frank had seen her first, and before she lit into him, he took the lead.

"Afternoon, ma'am," he said, smiling broadly. "See you met my cousin, Ian, here. Good man. Quiet. Clean. Works hard. Like me. We won't be no trouble at all. We been out'n the woods cuttin' timber. Now we rest 'n clean up. Your husband do this work?" He grabbed the rough staircase and shook it to demonstrate its strength. "A fine job. Sturdy." Everyone looked at him, bewildered. "Strong," he tried to explain.

Then the old woman started in again, this time on Frank. But he couldn't understand a thing and assumed that she couldn't, or wouldn't, understand him either, so he turned back to the old man and said as politely and quietly as he could, "Better rein your wife in a bit, man. We don't need much a' this."

"Mother," the man corrected, starting to laugh. "Mother." Then he turned to her and mumbled something in Finnish, and she too started laughing and turned back to Frank, this time with a trace of smile in her eye. She said something he couldn't understand but took to mean she was no longer angry. Frank wondered if this was some kind of test that she put all prospective roomers through. He made a gesture excusing himself. "Come on now, Ian," he said. "It's growin' late. We gotta be off."

"Mmmmh, money," the Finn grunted.

When the two stepped out onto the damp sawdust street, it was almost dusk, with a dank gray coolness edging toward frost. They walked crisply along, barely noticing the warm supper smells that leaked from the houses they passed.

"Can y' beat that!" Frank blurted. "She's his mother. Here I thought they was married and it turns out she's his mother. How auld y' figger him? Forty? Forty five? No more'n forty five. You see those arms? Hell, he was one tough logger in his day, I'll bet. But look at 'im now. Aye, livin' down here in Finntown, grubbin' for nickels and waitin' to die. That's Maki in five more years. That's any dumb swamp rat that stays and works for these maggots. But it ain't me, and it ain't you either. You 'n me, we're gettin' out of this dump, eh. First thing come morning, we get us a wagon. We get us a team. We get some supplies. We get outta this swamp. It's Oregon for us. Eh?"

"What's that?"

"What?"

"That noise."

"Sounds like trouble."

Now they were running, unaware of anything but their caulked boots spitting sawdust and the anger pulling them forward. It sounded like a fight, and Frank was ready.

"Somethin' about pay!" Frank shouted as they got close

enough to pick out individual words and voices. "Somethin'
about we ain't gettin' paid!" Every logger knew of jacks who
had worked all winter out in the swamps just to learn the company was broke, or claimed to be, and couldn't pay, or would-
n't, except in scrip, which could only be spent at the company
store. No one had heard of its happening in Menominee, but
it had happened nearby. It could here.

Chests heaving, boots heavy, they slowed and stopped.
Out front of the Continental building, Frank saw his camp-
mates, about twenty-five, clustered in a small, noisy group.
They shook fists and yelled at Culhane, who stood by a dark
suited man on the building's front steps.

"What in hell's goin' on?" Frank elbowed through the
crowd. Excitement tightened around him, as though they had
all been waiting, as though they knew only he dared stand up
to the bosses, knew he'd get his pay—whatever it took. And if
he got his, they'd get theirs, too.

Frank didn't know how it happened, but there he was suddenly out front of the others, their anger now behind him like
a prod. He felt Ian standing strong beside him.

"Where's our pay!" he demanded.

"Shut up, McDonald!" Culhane ordered. "Mr. Garrison just
explained that. It's comin'. You'd a kept your pants shut a
minute longer and come in with the rest of us, you'd know that.
Ask them. They know." He gestured at the men, implying they
had already accepted a deal. They shouted back their denial.

"I'll hear it from him!" Frank pointed at Garrison. He recognized him now as the man who'd hired him on that first
year, the snapping turtle. "Let's hear him say it."

"All right, you men! All of you! Listen!" The authority in Garrison's voice surprised Frank. It froze the whole group. Then, once it captured their attention, the voice grew quieter, more deliberate. "I'll explain one last time for everyone. We're closed. This is Saturday. I'm late for an important engagement. We shouldn't have held the office open today in the first place. It costs the company money. Now it's after five o'clock. You've come in when I have no help and the records are put away. And you want your pay now. Well, I have it—inside. But I have an important engagement. I'm already late. I can't call everyone back. But I understand. You want your pay. And you've earned it. It's been a long winter. You've done a good job. So I've authorized Mr. Culhane to advance you each five dollars, with the balance to come first thing Monday morning when we open our doors for business."

"Okay, boys! You heard him! Line up over here!" Culhane called out.

"Monday morning! T' Hell with Monday morning! I won't be here Monday morning!" Frank stepped directly up front of Culhane and stared him in the eye. "That's number one. Number two: He ain't got it. He's just stallin' while he thinks what t' do. This weasel"—he turned and jammed a finger into Garrison's chest—ain't got it!" The crowd let out a roar of agreement.

"You lousy shanty boy! You call me a liar?" Culhane stepped forward, spun Frank back around and pushed his chin into Frank's face.

"If he's got it, let him pay it." Frank said slowly, not giving an inch. "I don't trust a camp boss that turns his back on his

70

men, us that worked for him all winter, and sucks up to a weasel like this."

Without warning, Culhane's fist crashed into Frank's jaw, snapping his neck, sending him stumbling over backwards into the wet sawdust street. Above him, Frank saw Ian lunge forward—the clean silver blade of his knife flashing toward Culhane's throat, and then the scene dissolved in a tangled web of legs and caulked boots above him, until he saw Garrison, apart from the rest, pressed up against the building. That's when Frank realized it wasn't Culhane he wanted anyway, but the snapping turtle, the one that pulled Culhane's strings—the big boss.

In one long, liquid movement, Frank sprang forward across the gap that separated them. His fist crashed hard into the arc of Garrison's nose, and he felt the man crumple. Even as he slumped, Frank grabbed him and pulled him back up, staring for an instant into his terrified eyes.

"You pay me now or I kill you." Frank spit the words one at a time into Garrison's face.

But Robert hung limp in his hands, a sack of flour. He gave no response. Frank shook him, then, lifting him off the ground, began smashing his head into the wooden wall. "Give it, you sucker! Cot tamn, you give it!" he shouted.

And then everything went blank.

George

GEORGE NEEDED HELP. Not five minutes ago when he waded into the crowd brushing loggers aside with his rifle butt, but now as he looked up from Frank, who lay crumpled at his feet, to Garrison, who stood white and shaking in front of him, a trickle of blood running from his nose. The deputy wanted Ruprecht there.

"All right!" he shouted. "That's enough!" But he didn't know what to do next. Someone had to go to jail. He saw that, and it couldn't be Garrison or Culhane. He could see that, too. "All right, Mr. Garrison," he finally said, "I got 'em quiet now. You tell me what happened."

"This man!" Garrison pointed at Frank. "He attacked me. He threatened to kill me. And that one!" He pointed at Ian. "He went after Mr. Culhane with that knife. It's a wonder we aren't both dead."

"That right?" the deputy asked Culhane.

"You heard it. That one there tried to kill Mr. Garrison, and the dummy here came at me with a knife. Came right for my throat."

"Nay, nay! Tell it right, Culhane!" Frank challenged, climbing back to his feet. "Tell him how we didn't get paid! Aye, then tell him who took the first swing!"

"That right?" George asked.

"Now just one minute, deputy," Garrison interrupted. "You can't believe I intended not to pay these men. The idea is absurd. I was merely explaining our weekend salary disbursement policy. I assured them in the strongest terms that they would be paid in full on Monday morning and would immediately receive a five dollar advance against wages, when these two thugs rose up. They tried to kill us. They are dangerous. Lock them up before they do some real harm."

"Okay, you two, follow this." George poked Frank in the ribs with his rifle barrel, prodding him toward the jail. Though unconvinced by Garrison of any real danger, the deputy couldn't see much choice but to go along. Yet once the loggers saw where this was headed, they let out a howl and tightened in a line between George and the jail. Both sides watched, waiting for the deputy to move. Both sides seemed right, yet both looked wrong. George was caught in the middle. And then he saw Ruprecht.

The sheriff stood alone, down by the corner, one foot up on the boardwalk, arms folded over his chest, just watching. George felt him smirking, as if to say—"See, I said you couldn't handle my job, and you can't." But he didn't have to say it with words. He puffed up his chest, threw his arms down loose at his sides, and stepped up onto the boardwalk and then onto the porch as though it was a stage. His good eye burned into George's forehead, while the glass one rolled bizarrely off toward Culhane.

"All right," Ruprecht said, "let's hear the story. You first, George."

So, George told the story, careful to get all the details straight—what he had seen, what he had heard, from whom. "So, I was gonna haul these two in and cool 'em down some when I seen you comin' up there and says to myself—'Hold up, George. Here comes the sheriff. He'll wanna handle this his own way.'"

Ruprecht nodded noncommittally. "Only thing I don't understand is how all this fightin's gonna get anyone paid or back home any sooner." He looked at Garrison. "Don't look like anyone's hurt too bad yet. But these men feel pretty strong about gettin' paid. You wanna end this thing fast, you better pay em."

A roar of approval went up. Garrison's face tensed. His gaze met Ruprecht's. "Do you mean to stand here and tell me straight out that you're turning this town over to mob rule? Do you mean to say that any time a mob gets together and tries to turn order and justice around, you will go along? Will you really stand by while cutthroats attack decent citizens, then reward the attackers and punish the victims! Has it gone that far?"

"I ain't gonna argue this now. You just pay up and we'll have it out later. This ain't the place."

"Your own deputy saw it." Garrison turned toward George. "You saw what they did. You were about to drag these two thugs off. You tell him."

The deputy stood stock still.

"That's enough!" Ruprecht burst out. "I'm the law here. Nobody else. Not you. Not these men here. Me. Nobody else." He looked around, first at the crowd, then at Frank and Ian, finally at Garrison, for someone to contradict him. The air was silent till his eyes met Garrison's.

"Law? What law? Your law? The law of the jungle. This town hasn't had any law since you've been here, Ruprecht, and everyone knows it. Sober up and face facts."

Now Ruprecht was trembling. His lip and left cheek twitched. George had never seen him like that.

"If you got that money," Ruprecht said, "you better get it out here 'n pay these men their wages. If you don't, you better beg me to lock you up so they don't tear you apart."

Garrison turned toward the door.

"Want me to line 'em up out here or send 'em inside?" Ruprecht asked.

"Out here. It's still clean inside," Garrison snapped. "Come on, Culhane. I'll need some help."

George watched the pair disappear inside. The crowd's mood had changed. They had done it. They had won. They were getting their pay. The air was light, almost festive.

"Now, you two!" Ruprecht roared, quieting the crowd, forcing attention to Frank and Ian. "This town don't need your kind. You understand? You're lucky this time. Nobody got hurt too bad, so I'm lettin' you go. That's right, lettin' you go. Can't see I got much to hold you on. But there better not be a next time! Understand? Because if there is, me 'n George here, we gonna lock you boys up with a crazy Indian we got over there, 'n you just might not come out breathin'. Understand?"

"Hey," Frank began, "we wasn't . . . "

"You understand what I'm sayin', boy!"

"Sure, I do, b . . . "

"Then you shut your damn fool mouth 'n you do what I say!"

"Hey, out there!" Culhane's voice boomed. "Somebody grab th' other end a this table."

"Grab it, George," Ruprecht ordered. The deputy stepped over to the door, where Culhane was trying to wrestle a big maple table through a too-narrow opening. Inside, the deputy saw Garrison standing, waiting for them to clear the way. Under his arm he clutched an account ledger. Beside him on the floor sat a strongbox. He had somehow found time to re-comb his hair and clean most of the blood from his face, but beneath his nose, his left hand held a bloodstained handkerchief. At last the three men turned the table on its side and maneuvered it outside, two legs at a time. Then Culhane went back in for the strongbox and a chair, which Garrison unceremoniously slumped down in and opened his book.

"Take care a these two first," Ruprecht said. "I'm runnin 'em on outta here now, before they get into real trouble."

"Why should they make more trouble when you give them whatever they want?"

"Just what they got comin'," Ruprecht said, looking at Garrison. "Just like everyone else." He turned toward Frank. "You! What's your name?"

"McDonald."

"Frank?"

"Mmmhmp."

"Make your mark here."

"You?" Ruprecht demanded of Ian while Frank bent over

the table. "You! What's your name?" Ian made no move to respond.

"That's my cousin, Ian. Ian McDougall."

"Let him talk," Ruprecht said. "What's your name, boy?"

"Ian," came the hesitant reply, "Ian McDougall."

"No Ian McDougall listed on the payroll," Garrison snapped.

"What in hell?" Frank yelled, starting toward him. "You can't pull that. He's been out there all winter, same as me! You can't . . . "

George, seeing Frank start forward, jammed the rifle barrel into his gut. But the logger's stomach was solid, and the gun didn't sink in far. It was hard not to pull the trigger. Then he felt the rifle being knocked aside, and he wished he had shot. His eyes met Frank's in a quick, cold exchange.

"Cut the games, dammit!" Ruprecht ordered, looking at Frank. "You won't get nothin' but trouble like that." The deputy felt the words were meant as much for him as for the logger, and that made him even madder—not just at Frank, but at the sheriff, too. "Let's get this settled," Ruprecht went on. "You!" He looked back at Ian. "What'd you say your name was? Speak up this time if y' want your pay!"

"McDougall," Ian mumbled even less audibly than before, "Ian McDougall."

"I'll teach him how to talk," George volunteered, raising his rifle so he could bring it down across Ian's head.

"You just settle down, George. I heard him. I heard him. I got a job for you here in a minute."

"Nothing has changed," Garrison replied, "We still have no

Ian McDougall listed here on the payroll."

"Here, let me see that book there," Ruprecht said brushing around Culhane to the back of the table. He ran his finger down the column of names. "It must be this one," he said. "This John McDonald here."

"Aye," Frank shouted, "that's him. He goes by that sometimes."

"Okay, McDonald." Ruprecht looked at Ian. "Get over here 'n make your mark."

George watched the brief transaction without interest. He was waiting to see what Ruprecht wanted him to do.

"Now you boys got your pay, you get outta town," Ruprecht said. "You get on t' wherever you're goin'. I don't care what you do. But just one thing. Don't ever come back here again. You understand?"

They both stood silently, giving no sign.

"You understand me!!??" Ruprecht shouted. George leveled his gun on a spot between Ian's eyes.

"Yeah," Frank replied carelessly. "We understand."

"How 'bout you? George demanded, pressing the rifle barrel against Ian's forehead, "You understand?"

Ian said nothing.

"He understands you," Frank replied.

"Let him say it."

"That's enough, George. Let 'im be. That dummy can't do nothin' without his brother anyhow. Just get them out of here. Now which way you two headed?"

"Back east. Back up the Soo," Frank replied quickly.

"Grab your gear then 'n get movin'. George, you follow 'em

out a ways. Make sure they go."

George stuck close behind, poking them in the ribs as they walked to the wagon where their gear was stowed. This wasn't quite what he had hoped for. He'd hoped for a chance to really lay into one of them, especially the big dummy. But at least he'd have them alone for a while. Maybe they'd try to escape.

"Come on, swamp rats," he said, poking Ian again with the rifle. "I ain't got all night."

Ruth

"I'M SORRY, MARY DEAR," Ruth whispered, pulling a blanket up around her daughter's shoulder. "It must have been very important, or Daddy would surely have been home long ago. Why, he invited Reverend Goodwin, himself. You know how he was looking forward to this meal, all of us there together. But we can't always do as we like in this life. Your father works hard. He works hard for all of us. He works hard, because he loves us." It was speech she made often, with slight variations. She couldn't say where she had learned it, maybe in church, or maybe her own mother had whispered those same words to her as a girl. Maybe she had first put them together that way herself without thinking about it, or maybe Robert had taught her to say them. She couldn't have said, but she knew how she hated to repeat them.

Unconsoled, Mary rolled over and buried her face in the puffy down pillow. Tonight, though, Ruth lacked the patience to continue making excuses. The Reverend still waited downstairs for Robert, who hadn't returned though the clock had long ago chimed eight. She turned out the lamp. She kissed her daughter lightly on the cheek, tucked the blankets up around Mary's neck, and straightened back up. She sighed slightly and went out the doorway, then turned her head back into the room.

"Daddy will be home with us tomorrow," Ruth said. "All day." She wondered how much of Mary's disappointment was real and how much an act to gain sympathy. The children saw so little of Robert. He was home so seldom, and when he was home, he was always so distant, so preoccupied, especially these past few weeks, with the season ending. Still, he was their father. They needed his attention, his guidance, his love.

He shows us his love in his work, Ruth thought. It had to be true. It *was* true. There could be no other explanation, she assured herself. She took a deep breath to compose herself. Then she went down to meet the Reverend.

As she entered the parlor, Goodwin stood, his back to her, bent over slightly, one arm behind him, the other held up to the bird cage, coaxing Samson to perch on his index finger, which he had inserted between two thin golden bars.

"This is so embarrassing," Ruth said. "I can't imagine what's kept Robert so late. He can't have forgotten. It was the last word on his tongue last night and the first again this morning. He was so looking forward to this. I do hope there hasn't been some sort of trouble."

"Robert is an important man. Many others depend on him," Goodwin replied without looking away from the cage. "And this is an especially difficult time for him, with the crews coming in and the mill getting into full swing and so much else on his mind. No, I'm sure he hasn't forgotten. It isn't like Robert to make an engagement and then forget it. I'm sure he'll be along any minute now."

But Ruth wasn't so sure. In fact, after the strange way Robert had come home last night, she couldn't help worrying. So many frightening people came into town this time of year.

Goodwin turned away from Samson and looked up at her, smiling.

Ruth felt something peculiar about the Reverend, too—about his smile. She began to feel nauseous again, as she had a moment earlier after tucking Mary in. Something was wrong. She could feel it. Something important was going wrong, and Robert was involved. Something secret, and Reverend Goodwin knew about it, probably knew where Robert was right now. Goodwin's eyes met hers for a moment, but they gave away nothing.

"Yes," he repeated, "I'm sure Robert will be along any minute now." He didn't appear worried, just a trifle uneasy, as though he wanted to raise a point, but couldn't find a way to put it into words or introduce it into the conversation so he went on about something else. Before, it had always been Ruth with the heavy secret. Goodwin had always been so quick and easy with the answers, so optimistic and reassuring, but tonight she felt uncertainty behind everything he said—not fear or worry—uncertainty, lack of conviction. The whole evening had an eerie remoteness, as though they were both inexperienced actors thrown suddenly on stage in an unfamiliar play, and not only actors but playwright and audience as well.

"I'm in no hurry," Goodwin said. "You and I haven't spoken for some time, and I've been home alone all day, at work on tomorrow's sermon. So it is good to have this time now to visit."

She could think of nothing to say. An uncomfortable intimacy hung in the air, as though a critical meaning was about to be revealed, but each expected the other to reveal it.

"You have a beautiful home, a loving family. You have much to be thankful for," Goodwin said.

"Yes," she replied unconvincingly, "I have." But she couldn't say more. He lowered his eyes slightly, perhaps unconsciously. She felt his line of sight move across the curve of her breasts. Then he met her eyes again.

"I always feel such warmth, such love in your home when I visit. I am always reminded of why home and family are the cornerstone of the church. Truly, they are among the greatest blessings we can receive in this lifetime. In fact, that is the topic of my sermon tomorrow. 'Better to marry than to burn,' Paul said." He smiled hopefully. "Those words, so poignant, so profound."

"And yet you have never married," she observed casually. She knew she was fortunate in many ways, and she would even allow that it was good to be reminded of it now and then. But what, really, could the Reverend know of her life? How could he know what it was like?

"Oh, no," he laughed. "I'm afraid marriage wouldn't do at all for me. My life belongs to the Lord. I wouldn't make much of a husband."

Ruth knew she should say something, but couldn't. Every response felt inappropriate. And so the minister's words just hung for them both to consider. The silence deepened, and she saw that he, too, was embarrassed by the sudden air of uneasy intimacy.

"No," he finally reflected, "I lead a quiet life, a contemplative life, a life of service to the Lord and to my fellow man. I deny myself many things. Things other people take for granted. But I have no regrets. This is my calling. This is my life. My reward is in my service."

He lowered his eyes again slightly and then turned back toward Samson. He reinserted his index finger between the bars, but the bird still wouldn't mount it. Indifferent, Samson stayed firmly perched on his small swing at the top.

"I don't mean to be so somber and grave about it," Goodwin went on. "I only mean that when I come into your home and feel this warmth and love, I realize the weight of the cross I have been called to bear. I realize what I have denied myself. But I have no regrets, for I know I am doing His will. Why, look at Samson here. Even he would sing a sweeter song with a mate to keep him company." The Reverend was smiling easily now, and Ruth, sensing that he wanted to lighten the mood, relaxed a little.

"What?" she asked playfully, "A Delilah?"

"Ha. I should hope not. But even Delilah was an instrument of the Lord. 'And Samson said, "Let me die with the Philistines." And he bowed himself with all his might; and the house fell upon the lords, and upon all the people that were therein.'"

"Is that your meaning, then?"

"Why, yes. In a sense it is. Doesn't each of us have a purpose ordained by the Lord? Can even the basest, most wanton sinner obstruct His will?"

"Then we all may do as we please, if everyone does His will?" she bantered.

"Of course not. No. You know I don't mean that. What I mean to say is that we must be strong in faith, stand firmly with the Lord and follow the path that He, in his infinite wisdom, has chosen for us. And those whose faith means the most to Him are often put to the strongest trials, but if our faith remains strong, we have nothing to fear from anyone. That is my meaning."

"I just can't imagine what's keeping Robert," Ruth blurted. "This isn't like him at all. He's always so prompt about things. You must be starved, and by the time we're ready to eat the roast will be all dried out. I hope he's all right. With all these dangerous people in town. You don't think . . . "

"No," Goodwin broke in. "I don't. He'll be along any minute now with a perfectly good explanation."

Just then, Ruth heard some heavy footsteps out front on the porch. She stepped toward the door, but before she could reach out, it flew open in her face.

"Oh, Robert!" she screamed, gaping at his swollen nose and the bloody handkerchief he held beneath it. "Oh, my God, Robert! What have they done to you? What have they done?"

Ian

WITHOUT BREAKING PACE, Ian shifted his duffel to his left shoulder. They were about three miles east of town, and he wanted to rest, but if he slowed even a little, he felt the deputy's rifle barrel poke the center of his back.

"All right," George said finally. "Here's where I stop. You two keep movin'. Down around that bend there. This gun can reach that far."

Ian looked down to where the dirt road curved away into shadow. On either side grew tall hard woods, beech and maple, which, not yet in demand, had been left standing. He no longer heard the deputy's footsteps behind him, only Frank's on his left. Frank grunted once, shifting his load, but neither spoke. Nor did they slow down.

And they didn't look back to see what George was doing. Ian knew without looking that the deputy had his sights set on their backs. He thought he could feel the aim move back and forth between Frank and him. He felt a steady, yet barely noticeable pressure on the back of his head. But sometimes it lifted for a moment, and he knew then the aim was on Frank. He wondered if Frank felt it shifting. But he didn't ask.

He wanted to reach that dark spot where the road curved

around toward Lake Michigan, out of rifle shot, to sit and rest on a stump. He shifted the pack to his right shoulder again and enjoyed an instant of relief before it dug back into its familiar groove. He felt the earth turn beneath his feet like a rolling log or a treadmill upon which he had to move at just the right speed or be thrown over backwards into a gun barrel, but the bend didn't get any closer. He had to keep going forward just to stay in one spot, and all the time he felt the gun's pressure, lifting and coming back, lifting and coming back.

Then he reached the bend and knew in a few more steps he'd be out of sight, and so he turned, and as he did two sharp cracks split the air behind him. The dull thunk of a slug hit a nearby tree. Imagining where the second slug had gone, Ian looked around at his cousin.

"Let's sit down here and rest a minute," Frank said. "He'll head back t'town soon."

Ian eased the pack from his shoulder. He sat beside it on the dirt road and began to knead where it had been digging into his muscles, first the right side and then the left. He didn't feel much like talking, but he knew he would have to.

"You figure we'll see Birch Creek tonight?" he asked.

"Ah nay, we got ourselves a place to stay, haven't we? Back there in Menominee."

Ian didn't like what he was hearing. He remembered some things the sheriff had said, and the deputy's rifle. "You mean you're going back?"

"You mean you ain't?"

"That town," Ian said, turning the word over in his mouth,

searching out reasons he knew Frank would demolish. "It's got too much hate."

"I guess you ain't hungry then. How long since you ate? How long till you'll see any food out here on the road? How long?"

Ian shrugged his shoulders. He was hungry.

"How long since you had a bath or a woman?" Frank went on. "You won't find them out here either, now will you?"

"I guess I can last a while," Ian said. Food was essential. A bath and a woman sounded good, too, but he hadn't had either in so long he figured he'd get by a few more days, as he had all winter.

"Then what y' gonna do? Go on back home to the farm? Hitch yourself up to the plow? What about Oregon? What about the rest a your life, eh? Nay, y' can't turn back now!"

"You mean we ain't headed home?" Hadn't Frank told the sheriff they were going home? Wasn't that why Ruprecht headed them back east? "You told that sheriff . . ."

"To Hell with the sheriff. One-eyed fool don't see nothin'. I don't care about him. First thing come mornin' I'm off for Oregon. But right now I'm gettin' a bath 'n a good meal 'n some a that sweet, sweet woman love back there."

"Won't find nothin' but trouble back there."

"You figure he's gone yet?"

"Who?" Ian asked.

"That deputy."

"Might be."

Frank stood up and walked a few steps back down the road to where he could peer around the bend. "Hell!" he said, "He could be back there anywhere, just hopin' we come back, just waitin' to blow our heads off."

"It's crazy t' try. You know they'll be watchin' out for us. You heard what they said."

"Aye, they'll be watchin' the road. We can circle around by the lake 'n follow the shoreline back. They won't think about watching the beach, now will they? We can keep off the streets. Besides, it's dark enow t' move easier. We just go back to our room and then bang—first thing come morning we get us across t' river 'n into Wisconsin. Sheriff won't bother us there. We find us a team, we find some supplies, and we're gone before they ken a thing."

It was clear Frank had made up his mind, and Ian had to admit it sounded like a good plan, better than going back along the road anyhow. Then too, he could feel his stomach tightening. It was on Frank's side. They had no food, and it could be almost daylight before they reached Birch Creek.

"Well, sae be it, then. I guess we hafta try it then, don't we?" he said standing and hoisting his pack. He looked over at Frank, who was heading off into the trees for a place to cut through to the beach.

"Here we go, Ian," he shouted back over his shoulder. "I found us an opening."

Ian balanced the pack a little better. Then followed his cousin off into the woods.

89

Garrison

ROBERT LIFTED A BITE of mashed potato and examined it a moment. Even the gravy looked dry, as grey and tasteless as everything on his plate. He'd forced each bite down to his tightly knotted stomach. He set the potato back untouched and looked over at Goodwin, about to spear a small pearl onion—the last bit of food on his plate. Ruth had already finished. She was anxious to clear the table and bring on dessert.

"We've more of everything. Don't hold back," she offered.

"Oh, my goodness, no," Goodwin replied, daubing his lips with a stiff-white, lace-bordered napkin. "No thank you. I fear I've made a glutton of myself. But oh my, such wonderful cooking. I can't say when I've had better."

"I'm afraid it was all too dry," she apologized, looking at Robert's half-full plate. "I tried to keep it moist for you, but . . ."

"No, Ruth." Robert sensed her embarrassment. "It wasn't dry at all. It's just that I can't eat. My stomach is all in knots." He watched her gaze focus on his swollen nose. There was an awkward moment of silence.

"Of course," she said. "I hope some layer cake will soothe your nerves. It's your favorite—white with white frosting. And I'm sure it hasn't dried out." She started to rise.

"No," Robert said. "No, thank you. Not now, I couldn't enjoy it." He knew she'd be hurt that he refused dessert. He kept his eyes on the table, even after she removed his plate.

"And you, Reverend Goodwin?" she asked. "It's really very light."

"Oh, Ruth, you know I'd love to, but I'm afraid I just can't."

"Just a small piece?"

"Now, Ruth," he repeated, "you know how I love your cake, but I'm afraid I may over-indulge. And besides," he went on, "I think it should be saved for a time when we are better prepared to enjoy it."

"Then you'll take a piece home with you?"

"Ah yes, of course. That will be just the thing to inspire me while I put the finishing touches on tomorrow's sermon." He set his napkin on the table and smiled warmly.

"I guess you two don't think it matters if the law has no meaning anymore, if it has fallen into the hands of savages, animals, cutthroats."

"On the contrary, Robert, I quite agree. It's a shame. It's a tragedy. It always is when passions overflow."

Robert took the remark as a veiled reference to last night's crisis.

"Nevertheless," Goodwin went on, "I can't imagine how Ruprecht could justify setting them free after they assaulted you and Mr. Culhane. What could have possessed him? What is a jail for if not men like that?"

"*Men*? You call them *men*? Those animals? Those aren't men! Their grandchildren won't be men. Have you seen how they live? The filth? The stench? The lice? I have. Have you

heard them? The vulgarity! The drunkenness! The . . . The . . ."
As Robert searched for the word, he saw Goodwin's alarm and
realized he'd been shouting. Ruth stood frozen in the kitchen
doorway, a silver tray full of dirty dishes.

"But they *are* men, Robert," Goodwin replied. "That's pre-
cisely the point." Then, tipping his head slightly, "Perhaps we
should talk in the parlor where we won't be in Ruth's way."

Ruth retreated back into the kitchen, and the two men rose
from the table.

"I must say, Robert, as a man of the Lord I'm alarmed just
as you are by these recent events, perhaps more so. Still, I'm
not entirely surprised. When men forget the words of the Lord,
they are capable of the meanest, most repellent acts. And yes,
they may behave like animals, indeed worse than animals, but
always, in His eyes, they are men."

Robert started to lose track of what Goodwin was saying.
It was too theoretical, too abstract. It didn't connect with the
pain in his nose or the pounding in his chest. Nothing but
words, Robert thought. He's nothing but words.

Goodwin went on. " . . . but inside every man is a soul, a
soul that yearns for truth, for light. And that light can only
shine forth from the Lord. It shines through His works and
through the faith and moral virtue of His followers. We must
let our lives so shine before others that . . . "

"It has to be more than that," Robert interrupted.

"What?"

"We must do something definite. Something to show this
town where we stand, to draw Menominee together against
this savagery. If we don't, the next few weeks could be bloody.

I fear for Ruth. I fear for my children."

"Are you suggesting a revival?" Goodwin asked.

"Well, yes. Yes, that could be part of it. But more than that, we need a new sheriff."

"What?"

"Yes. Ruprecht is a godless man, a lawless man. He takes the criminals' side consistently. A drunkard, a public fornicator!"

"A what?"

"That's right! It's a running joke in every saloon on Bayshore Street. He calls it 'making the rounds.' That's how he takes his payoff."

"No! But I had no idea!"

"It's common knowledge—the town's disgrace. No one respects a law like that. We'll never know decency or moral virtue until we remove that sheriff." Last night Goodwin had persuaded Robert to pledge his life to the Lord. Now, Robert was laying down his terms of service. If the two had formed a holy alliance against evil, Robert would choose the weapons— more than mere words.

"You're right, of course, Robert," Goodwin finally agreed. "But my concern is not so much with the enforcement of the law as with the health of men's souls. For if the soul is filled with grace, man's law will become the mirror of His. A man who is secure in his faith owes allegiance to the Highest Law, and when such a man lives and acts in this world, his every deed is a blessing and a glory to God. If we would make this town a better place to live, we must concentrate on winning souls. Why don't we talk to Ruprecht? Invite him to join us in our worship.

Seek him out. He sounds like an unhappy and lonely man. He, too, can be brought to the fold."

"Talk. Is that all again? We'll talk and we'll pray. That's fine. That needs doing. I know. But time comes we must act. Look at this town. We've been talking and praying for years, and it's worse. Something must be done. You can't save Ruprecht anymore than you can those animals who assaulted me, there in the center of town, on my office steps, in broad daylight! And where next time? Here, in my home? And even then, Ruprecht would release them. You can't talk to a man like that. Talking's not enough. Something must done before it's too late."

Goodwin walked to the window, where he stood looking up, and out, as though for guidance. From across the room, Garrison watched his heavily lined face, reflected in the glass—a somber, glistening image against the cold night sky.

"I suppose you're right," Goodwin said, turning around and looking Robert in the eye. "A man must stand up and act for what he knows to be right. Christ did when he drove the moneylenders from the temple. And now we're called to follow that example."

"Then I have your support on this?" Robert asked.

"Yes. You've convinced me we have no alternative. I'll support you in whatever way my position allows."

"Good. That's all I ask. That you use your influence to help replace Ruprecht. That you speak out firmly against this moral anarchy."

"Count on me."

"You don't know how it raises my spirits to hear you say so, Reverend, to know you haven't lost faith in me."

"Now, Robert," he smiled, raising his right hand. Garrison reflexively drew back a bit. Goodwin smiled understandingly. "The Lord is ever-living, ever-compassionate. Ask and you shall receive. Knock and it shall be opened." He paused, but Robert remained silent. "It's getting late now," Goodwin went on, withdrawing a watch from his waistcoat. "I truly must be on my way. I have some touches to add to tomorrow's sermon." He glanced toward the door.

"Of course," Robert said, helping him on with his overcoat. "Ruth! Reverend Goodwin must be on his way now." Ruth stepped out of the kitchen, taking off her apron.

"I want to thank you again, Ruth, for that delicious meal and also for our visit. I can't say which I enjoyed more."

"Thank you," she replied. Robert opened the door, but Goodwin didn't move. He looked at Ruth as if expecting more. Then her eyes brightened and she hurried back into the kitchen for his cake. He received it ceremoniously and at last took his leave.

Robert closed the door and turned back into the house. Ruth stood silent and expressionless. Their eyes met only for an instant. He glanced quickly down and away at the dining room floor. The question her eyes asked had grown too complex, as complex and deep as their life together. And deeper.

"I've finished in the kitchen," he heard her say. "I'll go up now."

"Yes," he replied after a brief silence. "I'll lock up and turn out the lights."

Frank

"NOW ALL I NEED'S A WOMAN," Frank laughed, rubbing his chin. He felt good. His plan had worked. He and Ian had circled back along the shoreline to town, where their room was still vacant and a warm meal ready. So they ate. And then they bathed—a deep, warm, soapy bath drawn up by the old woman. If it didn't get the lice out, it knocked them groggy because Frank couldn't feel them moving. Later he'd have time for a kerosene shampoo. Now, back upstairs, he sat naked on the bed, laughing and passing a whiskey bottle to Ian, who sat opposite him, but down more toward the foot. The whiskey wasn't bad. Frank bought it from the Finn after checking to see it hadn't been watered too much.

"Well, she's down there a waitin'," Ian muttered, looking up with a smile for Frank's response.

Frank picked up a pillow and tossed it at Ian. "Hell, I ain't that hard up yet." He took another swig. "She's more your style, eh."

"You ain't thinkin' about goin' out again?"

"Thinkin' about, hell! Ain't nothin' round here but you 'n that ol' lady, 'n she's too loose and you're too tight for me." Frank could see Ian didn't like the idea of going out again, but he wasn't worried. He remembered a place he'd gone the year before—out of town a way, off by itself in a low, swampy clearing. He was sure they could get out there and back without being seen. "Come on get them clothes on 'n we'll go. This'll be a cinch. Smooth as hell. You just follow me." He jumped up and threw on a shirt, the same one he had on before. It smelled pretty bad, and he wished he had a clean one, but he didn't. "Come on, man. Get somethin' on that horny hide a yours. It's time t' get you some pussy. Best you ever had." Frank puffed out his chest and tucked his shirt into his pants.

Ian stood and pulled on his own shirt. "I hope you know what you're doing."

Frank pulled his suspenders up over his shoulders. "You ever seen the time I didn't?" he asked, grabbing another swig.

Billy

"HE JUST KINDA WENT CRAZY," Burma mused, less to Billy than to herself. "He looked kinda scared or something, so I tried to relax him a little. I've seen some nervous like that before, but they always settled down and did just fine. I always send 'em off happy like Fanny says. But this one. He just exploded. I've never seen anything like it. He could've killed me."

"The bastard," Billy muttered looking up from the cards on the kitchen table. Burma was so attractive he found it hard to look at her for long. He felt so ugly and clumsy beside her he wanted to bury himself in the earth. But she talked to him. Talked to him like he mattered. Nobody else did. And the one time he came to her in bed, even though he paid just like the others, she was more warm and receptive than he'd ever dreamed possible. And how old had she said? Seventeen?

Sometimes she'd ask his advice about things, and sometimes she'd just tell him how she felt, or talk about her life. He didn't care what she said. He liked to hear her voice go on like that. The clear liquid sound didn't hurt like her looks. He could listen all day.

"Lily says to watch out because he'll have it in for me now, and he won't rest till he gets me run out of town. She says she's seen it before. But Fanny says, no. He won't be back."

"He won't be back. Not if I'm here. If he comes, I know what to do. Nobody gets past me twice. Specially him. Specially after what he done to you." He wanted to say more, but no words came.

Burma looked down, tracing a pattern like figure eights with her index finger on the tabletop. Her loose black hair fell like a veil across part of her face. Her neck was smooth and slender. Her skin dark.

"Well, it's a hell of a way to live," she sighed. "I'd like to get away from it. Everyone kicks you around. Uses you. Takes advantage. "

"Not no more. Not when I'm here. You just let me know. You just tell me. Between me and my brother, George, we can handle it. We run this town. That Garrison. He won't come back. If he does, I'll put him away." Billy couldn't understand how anyone could want to hurt her. What could you take that she wouldn't give freely?

She said nothing, as though her thoughts had gone off in another world, some faraway place she could visit in her mind, where things were different—warm and fluid. Soft. He felt a distance to her then, yet closeness too. Like she had conjured a special dream, a special place beyond words that he could almost envision. Yet she remained so remote and alone. He wanted to touch her, but didn't dare.

"Hell!" he said finally, trying to reach her. "I'm here, ain't I? You think I'd let anybody hurt you?" He pushed back his chair and walked to the pantry for the pistol. He took it out and whirled around. She kept looking at the table, but her finger stopped moving. He took aim on a spot about six inches in front of the finger, a place where the wood grain looked like a smeared-over target.

"Bam!" he shouted. "Bam! Bam! Bam! Bam! That's what I do to their heads, dammit! That's what I do to *his* head! You understand?"

"What the hell's going on out here?" Fanny shouted, bursting in from the dining room. Billy and Burma both gaped at her, as though caught by their mother in the cookies. "Billy, how many times have I told you to keep that damn thing put away where it belongs." Fanny took it out of his hand, and his face flared with shame. Then she stuffed it back into the pantry and turned away. "Come on now, honey," she coaxed, "we've got to be ready for guests." And she guided Burma to the door. "You get us a couple more bottles and bring them out," she ordered at Billy before vanishing into the parlor.

"Bitch," he muttered, raising his finger like a pistol toward the spot where her head disappeared though the door. "Bam," he said softly, "Bam. Bam. Bam. Bam." He walked over to the half-empty whiskey case by the back door and grabbed out a couple of bottles. Then he heard the dogs starting up, so he set the bottles on the table and went out to shut them up. Out on the stoop, he grabbed some wood, a few sticks up under his arm and one in his fist like a club, and stepped around to the dog pen.

"Shut up in there!" he shouted and chucked a stick at Buck, a powerful Alsatian. It thunked against his ribs. He crumpled slightly, but didn't squeal. And then Buck was back up against the side of the pen again, barking louder than ever now. Billy pulled out another hunk and cocked his arm again. Before he let it fly, though, he thought to look out and see what caused all the trouble. About halfway across the clearing, he made out two shadowy figures, not coming straight up the path like everyone else, but sneaking in from the west, straight out of the woods. Garrison, he thought. Garrison and that Frenchman come back to get Burma, but Billy didn't have the gun. He cursed Fanny silently, and then realized that the two were aware of him, had been watching him ever since he came out. He tightened his grip on the firewood.

He wondered if they had guns. If they had guns, they wouldn't pay any mind to the stick in his hand. It was no good to shout at them. No good to take out after them. If only he had that gun, it would all be different. And then he realized they were likely still hoping he hadn't seen them. He could trick them.

"Damn it, Buck, I told you to shut up!" he shouted into the dog pen. Then he cocked his arm and let fly again with the firewood. This time Buck shrank and whimpered slightly. The other dogs fell silent. Billy grabbed a few more pieces of wood and walked back into the house. As soon as he closed the door, he rushed to the pantry for the gun. It was there this time, loaded, almost warm in his hand as he ducked back outside. But no one was there. The dogs were all quiet in their pen. And no one was there.

Ian

H E STOOD IN THE OPEN DOORWAY, back a few steps behind Frank, who was talking to the big, dark-haired woman with the wrinkled face and the strange, slippery voice. The air was thick with small talk and smoke. Three other men he'd never seen before, and six or seven women were spread out drinking and laughing. He didn't like it. He wanted to be home in Quebec, or even back in town at the Finn's attic. He felt a drop of sweat running slowly down his side and pressed his arm up tight against himself to absorb it into his shirt.

"Come on, Ian," Frank called back over his shoulder. "Come on in and close the door. Can't let these lasses get cold, eh." A light ripple of laughter rolled out, as Ian reached around stiffly and closed the door. They were all watching him, waiting to hear his response. But he couldn't think of any. "How about some a that whiskey, Fanny?" Frank said at last, filling the silence.

"Couple of whiskeys it is, boys," she said, crossing to where a nearly empty bottle stood with some glasses on the sideboard.

"Hey, Sugar," Frank said to a tall, auburn-haired girl who approached them. "I'm Frank. This here's . . . " But he was cut off as the front door swung violently open, catching Ian from behind and knocking him forward into Frank. The room fell silent.

"Billy!" Fanny boomed. "What the hell are you doing, crashing in here like that?"

Ian spun around and saw the face, which reminded him of George. His hand went to his knife as he saw the pistol, waving in the air almost like a flag. It's the deputy, he thought. It's that deputy come after us with a gun. But the man brushed on by them as though they didn't exist.

"Prowlers!" Billy shouted. "Garrison and LaChance!" He reached out with his pistol and pointed it toward the door. "I seen 'em out there!" He waved the barrel close to Ian's nose. Frank hit Billy's arm, knocking the gun away.

"Best watch where you point that thing!" They were eyeball to eyeball now. Then Frank turned his head slowly toward Fanny. "No need t' worry, ma'am. That was just me 'n Ian here comin' cross the field. Then we saw your pimp there throwin' somethin', looked like wood, at your dogs 'n yelling. Then he comes bustin' in here wavin' that gun around. I guess we maybe scared him, didn't we?"

"Scared? You think you scare me, shanty boy? You don't scare me. Both you together don't scare me. I went back in to get my gun, and you're lucky you weren't still sneakin' around when I got back out there or you'd be one dead swamp rat— him, too, dammit!"

"Settle down, now, Billy," Fanny said, escorting him back to the kitchen.

"Settle down? What you mean, settle down?"

103

"I mean I want you back in the kitchen where you belong. I want you to stop bothering our guests here. And I want you to put that gun back in the pantry where it belongs."

"The pantry?" Frank asked. "You keep your gun in the pantry?" He tried to hold back a laugh, but couldn't. It came out slowly and spread, first to the other guests and then to the girls. Even Fanny smiled a little. "Then that white powder all over it—that's flour? Hey, pimp, you got flour on your gun?"

Even Ian chuckled a bit. The picture of Billy standing there, enraged and helpless, with flour all over his gun was so absurd he couldn't help it. Still, something in the way Billy looked at Frank made Ian shiver a little. He'd seen other men look at Frank that way, and he knew what it meant. Billy started forward, toward Frank, but Fanny stepped between them.

"That's enough, Billy! That's it, Billy!" she said, grabbing his arm like a disobedient schoolboy and ushering him to the kitchen. He allowed himself to be led.

"Maybe you should take away his bullets," Frank said.

Billy's head snapped around. Fanny pushed him through the door as the room convulsed with laughter. And then Ian noticed another one. Another one quietly watching. Another who wasn't laughing.

"Hey! Where's that whiskey?" Frank laughed, patting Lily on the ass. She went to the sideboard and poured the drinks.

But Ian was looking at someone else, the one with the delicate neck and the dark, quick eyes. She stood alone near the staircase. Once, he caught her looking at him, just for an instant, and then, almost before their eyes met, she looked away. He could see she was sad, and he knew why. He could feel how she hated the place, even more than he did. And he wanted to hold her, tell her he understood. He wanted her to know he was different, not like the others, that he'd be good to her—gentle, would take her away to a better place, a place where life was clean and good, a place to heal. Then, the auburn-haired girl was back, and she stuck a drink in his hand and gave one to Frank.

"You just get into town?" she asked.

"Aye," Frank said, impatiently. "Say, this here's my cousin, Ian. He don't talk much around strangers, specially the ladies. Whyn't you stay here and get t' know him a little. I see somethin' I need t' tend to." The dark-haired girl stood by the fireplace now, and Frank went directly to her—almost as though she was reeling him in on a line, but she wasn't even looking his way. Ian's chest got all tight and twisted.

"You two musta just got into town then?" Lily asked, stepping in front of Ian and partially blocking his view. But he looked beyond her, past the high nest of her hair, to Frank, standing now with his right arm on the mantel and his left in his hip pocket, talking to Burma. Ian wished he could hear what they said.

"Say, you don't talk much, do you?" she said. "Well that's okay. I guess I can talk enough for us both. That's what they say anyhow. Fanny's always telling me—'Lily,' she says, 'if you could get paid for talking, you'd be a rich woman right now.' Well, I guess I do talk a lot more than some of the girls, but"— she stroked his arm—"I do other things, too."

It was getting harder to ignore her, but he tried. He saw Frank running the backs of his fingers up and down the other girl's cheek. She looked down and slightly away. She has secrets, Ian thought, and so young. Frank can't understand someone like that. He'll be rough.

"I said I can do other things, and I bet you can too." Lily was rubbing on Ian now, her satin dress slippery across his wool shirt. Her lightly freckled chest became soft, white curves above the lace bodice. "Talking ain't the only thing in life," she observed. "Don't we know!" she added, rolling her eyes.

Ian studied her more closely. Though she, too, was young and attractive, her green eyes were puffy and tired from too much alcohol and sex in too short a time. He looked away again.

The dark-haired girl walked toward the stairs. Frank followed her with his eyes.

"You two been gettin' friendly?" Frank asked, walking back over to Ian. "You better watch out for him, Sugar. He don't talk much, but he's hung like a moose and twice as horny. Come on, Sugar, ol' Ian here's a hungry man. Whyn't you get on up t'ere 'n stoke up the oven a bit. He gave her a pat on the fanny. She smiled back at them and disappeared up the stairs.

"You got yourself a sweet one there, eh. Sweet, sweet sugar. A real man-pleaser. You see that little wench I wound up with? Burma, she says her name is. Tells me she's eighteen. Eighteen, hell! If she's eighteen, I'm thirty. Ah, shit. Who cares? Damn, I told y' this was the place t' come tonight. I could feel it. Just like Oregon. Didn't I know?" But before Ian could answer, Frank had started up the stairs. "Come on," he shouted back toward Ian, who had hardly moved since coming in, "Those things ain't got teeth."

Then Frank was gone. The other men had gone, too. Two women sat over on the couch, talking, unaware of Ian's presence. The kitchen door swung open. It was Fanny.

"Girls! Girls!" she scolded, looking at Ian. "Where are your manners? We have a guest here." The two rose almost as one from the couch.

"Uh . . . " Ian managed to mumble. He felt the blood rush to his face. "Uh . . . No . . . I mean I'm . . . " He looked up the stairs and pointed. They stared at him blankly. He turned away and hurried, almost stumbled, upstairs.

Goodwin

FOR SOME TIME NOW he had been lying awake in bed without spectacles, watching a hazy, half-circle of light thrown onto the ceiling by the oil lamp on his nightstand. It stretched and ran down the wall as though folded. Once, when the lamp caught a draft, the pattern twitched slightly, but otherwise it hadn't changed. Goodwin wasn't tired. He'd gone to bed only because he could think of nothing else to do.

Hours earlier, he'd come home eager to complete his sermon—

For they drank from the supernatural Rock
which followed them,
and the Rock was Christ.
Nevertheless, with most of them God was not pleased.
For they were overthrown in the wilderness.
Now these things are warnings for us,
not to love evil as they did.

All the way home, these words of St. Paul to the Corinthians had run through his head—so fitting, he thought. And when he arrived, he went straight to his writing table, pausing only to set down Ruth's cake and pull off his overcoat. He took up his tablet and studied what he'd written earlier that day. Though pleased with its general form and development, he now felt it lacked urgency, intensity. So he took up his pen and set to work, reinforcing patterns of repetition, sharpening metaphors, building alliterative bridges, making subtle adjustments in tone. And then he was done.

He paused, inhaled a deep breath and held it: "Let us pray," he exhaled, head lowered, eyes closed. Yes, it would work. In fact, it was perfect.

He rose and went to the buffet for his cake. Until now he hadn't examined it closely, he'd been so distracted. Four layers, white and moist, with the most extravagant and yet delicate icing he'd ever observed. This is how Ruth's sweetness and purity shine forth in all her works, he reflected. A sinful person could not make a cake like this. He went into the kitchen for a fork.

This was the first piece, he thought. She gave me the first and probably the biggest piece. And the way she looked at me. She wanted to tell me something. No, perhaps not.

He ate slowly, almost rhapsodically, licking his lips after each bite. At last, plate empty, he scraped up a final bit of icing with his fork, pressing a few neglected crumbs onto an outside tine, and cleaning them off with his tongue. He set the fork down and sighed.

Only later, as his thoughts turned to Robert, did the uneasiness return. No matter how Goodwin tried, he could not quite trust the man.

On the surface, Robert was sincerely repentant. And yet,

for all the display of remorse, something was lacking. More and more, Goodwin came to believe Robert planned to use him, the church, even God Himself, as tools of revenge. He thought again of Paul's words—

We must not put the Lord to the test,
as some of them did
and were destroyed by serpents,
nor grumble, as some of them did,
and were destroyed by the destroyer.

That was how he had gone to bed, yet now lying there on his side, knees curled slightly toward his chest, his sermon began to appear pathetic, foolish, almost naive. Exactly what Robert would expect.

Or *was* Robert sincere? *Had* he been truly changed? Goodwin wanted to believe so. It was a dark night full of tangled implications. Finally, he prayed for guidance. But no answer came.

Frank

H E FLOATED LIKE AN OLD, FLAT-BOTTOM BOAT, adrift before dawn
on the mirror surface of some half-remembered lake—a
fine mist rising and falling, as dew. Her stillness was the lake he
floated on, her dark liquid depth all under and around him,
inside him, as he was in her. So that to withdraw would be to
take *her* out of *him*, to become just Frank again—alone.

"Ahh, Burma . . . " he sighed, breathing deep musky smells
of broken earth, trying to lift his head. But failing, leaving his
face there buried in moist black hair, like silk but coarser,
more alive. He took another slow breath, held it deep in his
lungs, exhaled it at last with a moan.

Burma echoed his sounds, paced her breathing to his, and
Frank felt a mutual smile rolling out in ripples, so he lifted his
head and looked down at her face. Her eyes were closed. His
head was getting heavy. So he let it fall.

It's too long a time since I felt this peace, he thought. Too
long? maybe never. So many nights he'd dragged in from the
woods to camp, weary yet vaguely restless, a prisoner of sus-
picion and resentment. Hungry as he was, it could be hard to
get through supper. No talking allowed during meals, and the
primal sounds of men slurping, smacking their lips, scraping

knives and forks on their metal plates, had an eerie remote-ness as though from another life—not his. Yet he *had* stayed awake. Every bite of food—no matter how spoiled or foul-tast-ing—he ate, because it was fuel for his empty body. And when he could eat no more, he'd push to his feet and creak back through snow to his shanty, maybe get his boots off before falling into deep, dreamless sleep.

He'd been tired and he'd slept. But never in the past six months, maybe never in his life, had he known peace like this—and he was awake to enjoy it.

He ran the backs of his fingers along her cheek, noticed a nasty bruise on her left arm.

She trembled. He felt her muscles tighten slightly beneath him. Then he noticed the thin film of perspiration wherever their bodies touched—his chest, his belly, his outer thighs—and he knew it was over. Time to return to his life.

So he placed his palms flat out, one on either side of her head, and raised himself slowly—first his chest, then all down along his belly till he no longer touched her at all above the hips. Then, as the insides of her thighs began to fall away, he tensed his back and pulled his hips away slowly—so that he, so that both of them, though spent, though more than satisfied, could feel that last long second of their wholeness stretch like a slow strand of water before breaking apart.

Exhausted, he fell onto his back. A jagged crack in the ceil-ing ran like a lightning bolt into the far left corner above the door. Cool air began drying sweat from where they'd been pressed together. He closed his eyes.

"Frank? Her voice was clear, yet tentative, like a distant

bell. "Frank?" she repeated. He'd never before made love to a woman who called him by name. It had always been—"you big lumberjack," or "big fella," never "Frank." It felt strange to hear her call his name, as though she'd violated some unwritten rule of decorum.

"Nmmmmh?" he replied.

"I just wondered when you're leaving?"

"Leavin'! Leavin'? Can't y' be patient, I just . . ."

"No . . . " she laughed, "Not that. For Oregon. That's what you said downstairs. Or were you just talking?"

"Talk, hell! I say it, I do it. First thing come mornin'—come sun up—I'm gone."

"Just you and your brother."

"Aye, me 'n Ian. That's it."

"Then we won't see each other again." She sat up.

He watched the profile of her face.

"I know a girl went there once, to Oregon. Jeannie was her name. Took a train most all the way. Took a train from Duluth. Went to Portland." Burma tossed her hair back behind her, straightened her head, then looked him full in the face. "That where you're headed?"

"Could be," Frank said. "Near there, anyrode." He rolled over on his back again and put his hands behind his head. He looked up at the ceiling.

She stood quickly and stiffly.

"Hey, now," he said a little smugly, "you can't ask a man to change his whole life, just on account of . . ."

"Nobody asked you to change nothing," Burma cut him off. Turning her back, she pulled her kimono tight and walked

113

to the mirror, watched him over her shoulder.

"Well, what then? What's the quarrel then?"

"Nothing. Nothing's the matter. Everything's fine. Time to get dressed, that's all. Fanny'll want me back downstairs."

"Hey, look . . .." He stood and crossed to where she stood combing her hair. He noticed she was watching him in the mirror. "Here's how it is. Me 'n Ian, we had us some trouble back there in town. Not too bad, eh, but if they find we're around, they might lock us up. So we gotta go fast." They studied each other's image in the mirror. Her expression didn't change. "Hell," Frank went on, "I'd stick around if I could, wouldn't I?"

"Sure."

"Hey, look . . .," he tried again, hands on her shoulders, "I just don't want you t' think . . .."

"Think? Think what? I don't think. I don't feel. You don't feel nothin'. Neither do I. Everything's over. Nice and easy. You get dressed and get on your way. I got some things to do." She looked pointedly at the timer. "The sand's run out. Fanny doesn't pay me any extra for wasting my time like this."

Frank shrugged his shoulders and shook his head in exasperation, then walked back over to the chair where he'd thrown his clothes and began to get dressed. He hadn't thought about a train. He didn't know how far Oregon was, but he knew it was far, knew he had to cross forests and prairies and mountains and deserts. He knew what she wanted him to say, and he almost wanted to say it. She could be good company.

And not just in bed. She was bright and spunky, with a

quick, aggressive way of going after what she wanted. He liked matching up with her. She was almost sharp enough to twist him around and get him to ruin his whole life making her happy. Almost, he thought, but not quite.

He watched her now as she stood combing a few last tangles from her hair, just getting ready for another trick, like she forgot he was in the room, but nervous as a schoolgirl waiting for an invitation to dance. She's good all right, he thought, but no match for me. I read her like a map. I can beat her every time. And so he asked her.

"Look," he offered, "I gotta get outta here. That's it. Me 'n Ian. First thing come morning we're gettin' on t' Oregon. That's it. You want to come along—okay. But we gotta get out fast before that sheriff learns we're here. Get across that river t' Wisconsin. Maybe catch a train there, eh?"

She turned and looked directly at him.

"Well," he said finally. "You've heard it all now. Are y' coming along?"

"Oh, I want to. I need to. I don't know. I don't know what Fanny'll say."

"Fanny'll say? Ahh, who cares wha' Fanny says. We got no room for her anyrode. Y' comin' or no?"

"Okay," she sighed, as though giving in, as though she hadn't been hoping all along for him to ask. Then she laid down a condition. "But only if you can get Fanny to let me go."

"*Let* y' go?" Frank was astonished. "*Let* y' go? What the hell? She got no hold on you. If you got your mind set on't, there's nought for her t'do but wave bye bye."

"She can get awful mad sometimes."

"Sure, and so can I. I never yet seen a woman get madder than me," he joked. Then he looked her hard in the eye and said slowly, "Don't show 'er no doubt. She'll use it t' break y'. That's when you're done. So if you're not set on goin', if y' got any doubt, y' might as well say so now 'n save us all a mess a trouble."

"I'm set," she said.

"Then that's it. I'll take care a Fanny. You stay up here till I call. Then y' come doon—all packed up and ready t' go. Y' look at me—you don't even look at Fanny—and y' say, 'That's it, Fanny. You heard it from Frank.' Then y' follow me straight out the door."

"You think it'll work?"

"Sure, I know it'll work. No way can she stop us. You just start gettin' packed. We're goin' to Oregon."

She threw her arms around his neck and kissed him—a warm, girlish kiss. "I can cook pretty good, too," she offered.

"Well . . .." Frank reached back for his suspenders and pulled them up over his shoulders. He felt full again, strong. "If y' can't, it's a good time to learn."

Fanny

S HE SAT NEAR THE FOOT OF THE STAIRS in her platform rocker. Lily and three other girls clustered about the dining room table playing euchre. Unless you counted Billy—and Fanny didn't—Ian was the only man left downstairs. He sat alone, elbows on thighs in the center of the sofa, studying the rug.

"That brother of yours gets his money's worth," Fanny observed.

Ian looked up with an expression she took for surprise or mild amusement.

He made her uneasy. Not that he looked dangerous, but she was wary from yesterday. Her neck was still sore. And Ian just sat there, doing nothing, just fixed his eyes on something, anything—the rug, or a lamp—and stared in silence. Empty inside as a church at midnight, she thought. Just the opposite of his brother—always talking and jumping around like his blood's on fire. Like he thinks too much. And this one don't think at all.

Upstairs a door opened. Some heavy boots took a few deliberate steps down the hall. That's him now, she thought, as Frank's legs emerged from the shadows farther up the stairwell.

"Mmmmm! Hmmmm! Nothin' like good lovin' t' chase out those demons," he announced, his face all lit up.

Fanny knew it was true that nothing could improve a man's outlook on life like good hearty screw. Still, she mistrusted Frank, partly because of how he'd snuck in earlier, but mostly she felt he was play-acting, all that light talk and smooth manner contrived, a false front to hide something.

Ian started up from the couch.

"Hold up there, Ian," Frank said. "It's no hurry."

Ian stopped halfway.

"I got some good news," Frank went on, "for Ian, for Fanny here, and all y' fair ladies over there, too." He gestured expansively toward the dining room, where the girls stopped their game and focused on him.

The kitchen door swung open, and Billy poked his head out.

"Billy! You get back there in that kitchen. I don't want . . ." Fanny ordered.

"Ah, that's all right," Frank interrupted. "Let the pimp hear it, too."

Billy stepped into the room, the revolver tucked into his belt pirate-style. He stared hard at Frank, who kept on talking.

"That sweet angel up there . . ." Frank paused, adopting a voice of mock reverence, "has stole my worthless heart."

Everyone looked at each other. Was this a joke? Were they expected to laugh?

Billy and the girls looked to Fanny for guidance, but she didn't give any. She didn't like this a bit, but he was a guest, so she wouldn't offend him. She was just tired, and she wanted him to leave.

Billy, looking bored and disgusted, turned back toward the kitchen.

Frank didn't move.

He tries to play the clown, Fanny thought, but he's no good at it. Has to strain to be funny.

"Well, anyrode," Frank went on, "me and Ian here, we're leavin' for Oregon first thing tomorrow, y' see . . . 'n Burma 'n me, we got to talkin', and she says, 'We won't see each other again.' Simple as that, but it tore me up, so I says, 'Hell, Burma, why not just pack up your things 'n come along?' Why, you should 'a seen the smile . . . "

Fanny's monumental face froze. She knew Frank wasn't play-acting now. He meant this. Her hands tightened on the rocking chair arms till her knuckles bulged, but she didn't speak.

"So that's it," Frank continued, avoiding her eyes. "First thing come sun-up, me and Ian are off t' Oregon, 'n Burma's comin' along."

"The hell she is!" Fanny bolted up out of her chair, her face flushed with rage, her expression imperious as ever. "If you think you can stumble in here in the middle of the night and steal off one of my best girls you're crazy! You just turn around and march out of here now!" She pointed stiffly toward the door.

Frank took a half step toward her, but she didn't back off. She leaned forward slightly.

"Now settle down there a minute, ma'am" he said. "No need t' . . . "

"Settle down nothing! I'll settle down when you're out of this house and back in the hole you crawled out of! Oregon!? Why not the moon? You can sweet-talk her, but you can't

119

sweet-talk me. I take care of these girls! Good care! All of them! I give them a home, good money, a life! I don't let some lousy man, some shanty boy, some drowning swamp rat like you, grab hold of them and wreck their lives!"

"Now hold on a minute!" Frank shot back. "I'm not talkin' 'bout wreckin' nothin'. I'm talkin' 'bout gettin' outta this dump! I'm talkin' 'bout goin' someplace—Oregon! Burma already made up her own mind about that."

"Her *own* mind? What mind? Of course she wants to run away to Oregon. To Oregon or any other place with you or any-body else that'll take her. She's eighteen years old. What's she know what it's like out there in the world? What it's like to turn forty . . . wake up some morning and know there's noth-ing. Nothing left—no more good looks, no more man, no more money, no more food, nobody to turn to! Nothing! What's she know? Nothing! Don't you tell me, shanty boy. I know! I've seen it all! I take care of my girls. I teach them how to look after themselves."

"Aye, but it's her life, not yours now, ain't it?" Frank said firmly and flatly, like a lawyer resting his case. It was true, of course, and it enraged Fanny to think she might be beaten with this one point when all the rest of the arguments were in her favor, when she knew she was so obviously in the right.

"Besides, Burma owes me money!" she retorted finally, raising a point she'd hoped not to mention.

"Owes you money?" Frank looked back around up the stairs, obviously surprised.

"That's right," she replied smugly.

"How much?"

"More than you got." She saw Frank shoot a quick look over at Ian. "More than both of you, more than all three of you got put together! Plenty!" She knew she had him beat now, and though he wasn't quite ready to admit it yet, Frank sensed it too.

"Nay, she never said she owed money. Seems to me like you'd be the one owin' her. She works for you. Ain't that right? You pay her. She don't pay you!"

"I got my records," Fanny replied coolly. "Where do you think she gets those fine clothes? You think she makes enough to pay for them? I pay for them—real silk, some of them, fine lace—out of my own purse. Then the girls pay me back from their earnings. So don't you try to tell me. I got my records!"

"Why, you weasel. You lousy weasel." Frank's voice, gathering rage and intensity—but still hushed, barely a whisper— almost echoed. He stepped toward her. "Y' think y' can *own* someone!? Y' can't just buy a person like that! Y' can't own her!"

Then Fanny felt herself torn loose from the floor, like a leaf from a branch by the wind, and flying across the room until something hard and flat crashed into the center of her back. Then as she crumpled to the floor, she looked around and saw the girls spray back from the table in a clutter of lace and feathers. And Frank coming at her again.

And then came the blast—so loud it shook the walls. It hung in the air for a second, freezing all time and motion before fading, or twisting itself into a terrified wounded animal sound, only deeper—more human, and therefore more frightening.

121

And then, looking up, she saw Frank's face, contorted in shock and agony as he spun around sideways and, crashing over a chair, dropped face down beside her on the floor.

Billy

HEAD GIDDY WITH BURNT POWDER SMELL, he looked down at the revolver. A blue-gray smoke wisp curled up from the muzzle. His ears still rang from the shot. His arm still trembled from the jolt when he squeezed it off. His heart surged from seeing Frank crumple.

He raised the gun to his face, cradling it like a child with his left hand. And for that instant it was somehow more than a cold, mechanical device; it was an extension of his will, a function of his body, a conduit, a channel, into which he poured himself—poured everything he had ever been, had ever dreamed of becoming—in a single, overwhelming statement too pure, too perfect, too final for anyone ever to laugh at or ignore.

He didn't see the huge shape lunging toward him from over by the couch, not till it was nearly on top of him, didn't see the silver flash at all. But he felt the clean steel point drive deep between his ribs. Felt something like a log jam break up in his chest. And then, as Ian's knife tore through his heart, the room dissolved in a river of liquid color, and he felt himself being ripped by an unseen hand from this measured world of time and space into whatever it is lies beyond.

And that was the last thing he ever felt.

Ian

B ILLY LAY DEAD ON THE FLOOR. Fanny, half-prone beside him, didn't move. Her eyes fixed on Ian, who hadn't made a sound. His hand remained steady as he looked at the bloody knife. Then, reflexively, as though he'd just finished gutting a moose, he pulled the blade through the crook between his forearm and biceps, letting the still warm blood soak through his shirt.

He looked around slowly. Still nobody moved. Nobody but Frank, who squirmed in a circle on the floor, both hands clutched over the hole in his side. He made a low, gurgling sound like a drowning man gasping for air. Sheathing the knife again, Ian started toward his cousin, but his left foot came down on Billy's neck. He looked at the corpse a second then kicked it away.

"You okay." It was at once a question, a command, and a simple statement of fact. "We gotta go."

But Frank gave no sign he'd heard, made no motion to rise. He just kept gasping there on the floor, his body opening and closing like a jackknife.

Ian scooped him up like a child. Then, surveying the room, again, his eyes picked out Burma. Lavender coat on, carpetbag in hand, she stood at the foot of the stairs. He fixed his eyes on her as he crossed to the front door.

"You stayin' here," he said.

Burma looked up, straight at him now, in silence, then over at Fanny, at Billy's corpse. She tightened her grip on the carpetbag in her right hand. She shook her head, clearly and deliberately—No. "I can't stay here. Not now. Let me come."

"Nay. You stay here." Something inside him turned over like a cold, dead hand. Then he swung open the door and stepped into the night. The fresh air felt good on his face.

He looked across the open field to the distant line of trees, trying to find where he and Frank had emerged a few hours before, but unable to, he just started out, hoping his feet would somehow recall the way back to the Finn's place. When he reached the spot where Billy saw them earlier, he stopped to get a better grip on Frank and take one last look back at Fanny's house, to fix in his mind a picture of the place. As he did, he saw someone, one of the girls, burst out running toward them, her skirts and petticoats held high off the muddy ground. Frank was bleeding badly. His blood seemed to be everywhere. He still hadn't spoken.

Not quite in panic, though more hurriedly than before, Ian made for the woods, but as he began to run, Frank wailed out and his body began convulsing so bad Ian could barely hang on. Then, at last, he reached the spot where they'd emerged into the clearing, and so he stopped again and laid Frank at the foot of a small jack pine. He wanted to think.

At first, back inside, he'd acted without thinking, had known instinctively what to do. From the time the gun exploded till he stopped to look back at the house, he'd seen what needed doing and had done it. But now he began to doubt and second-guess himself. Back there, it was just a matter of getting away, finding a place to hide out while Frank recovered. But now he saw Frank would need help, and even with a doctor's care might not recover, and the future looked more and more like a bramble of doctors and jails—maybe that sheriff and his deputy again. Or else, or else what? Carry Frank on till he died? Leave him here to die? His own blood? The only friend he had ever had? His head pounded.

"Frank," he pleaded, "you gotta help me. You gotta tell me what to do next."

But Frank only made a low, indecipherable moan.

Ian lifted him again and headed back off toward Finntown. But the way wasn't easy. Coming here, Frank had led, breaking trail through the second-growth stubble, while Ian followed a step and a half behind. Now, carrying Frank, Ian stumbled through the maze of low, poking jack pine branches never quite sure of the right direction, coming out in a tangle of blackberry bramble, once losing his balance, almost falling on a patch of ice.

Frank's convulsions slowed and weakened. Where before there had been a wild electric energy all through his body, now he was aimless and heavy, hard to hang onto. As they came out of the brush, Ian was practically dragging him. He made his way east by moonlight, sticking close to the tree line until he was almost across from the Finn's place. Then he stopped and laid Frank down again while he tried to plan out the next step.

"Frank," he whispered, propping his cousin up against a low stump, so his head rested on top. Ian knelt low on one knee and leaned close to Frank's face. In his left hand, he held a piece of crusty snow, which he pressed on Frank's forehead, while he turned the head gently from side to side with his right. "Frank," he whispered again. Still no response.

Ian looked at the house, forty yards or so past an empty field on the far side of the street. It was completely dark. Remembering Frank had a front door key, Ian went through his pockets and found it. Now they would be all right. The Finns were in bed, and the street was empty. Ian would be able to let himself in and get Frank up to the room without being seen. He scooped his cousin up again, took a quick look into the field, and broke for the house. He got the door open quickly and dragged Frank inside.

As he stood in the darkened corridor trying to make out the ladder to the attic, he heard a door to his left creak open. He snapped his head around as a match struck and the room flooded with light. The old woman, the mother, held a bright lantern high in front of her broad face. She knit her brow as her eyes tried to adjust to the brightness. She first took in Ian, who stood directly in front of her, covered with dirt, sweat, and blood. Her eyes widened. Then she saw Frank slumped on the floor.

"Eeeeiayeeee . . . !" she screamed, cowering and turning away. Ian wanted to hide, to strike her, to stop the sound, but he didn't know what to do. And then her son was there, pointing her back to the bedroom, talking excitedly in Finnish.

Ian bent down to Frank again, trying one more time to shake him back to consciousness.

"He is alive?" the Finn asked suddenly.

Ian nodded.

"We take him to doctor. Come."

"Nay," Ian shot back. "We stay here. Doctor come here to us. You bring doctor here."

"No. We go to him. Now."

Not knowing what else to do, Ian pulled his knife from its sheath and held the still sticky blade close to the man's face.

"We stay," he said firmly. "You get doctor." This time the Finn nodded in agreement and headed back toward the bedroom, but Ian stopped him by pointing down at Frank with his knife, and then up the stairs at the attic. "You help first," he said, sheathing his knife and pulling Frank to the stairs. "Help first. Then go."

While Ian pulled from the top, the man got underneath Frank and pushed up on him, but that turned out to be the wrong way because whenever Ian pulled hard it put too much pressure on the wound, and the Finn wasn't strong enough anymore to be much help below. About all he could do was provide a bottom support level for Ian to pull from, and then he slipped or somehow lost his balance down there because Ian could feel Frank sliding out from his grasp and tumbling down on top of the Finn, which started him cussing, and the old woman, who had been standing in the doorway watching, screaming again.

"Stop!" Ian yelled, clambering down the ladder to help the Finn, who was himself soaked in blood now, get untangled from Frank. "Back up!" Ian ordered, and again they worked, the old man on top this time guiding and directing while Ian pushed and lifted from the bottom till they worked Frank up through the hole and out onto the attic floor. Now Ian came up through the hole, and he grabbed Frank again and dragged him over and dumped him on the bed.

"Now you get doctor," he told the Finn. "Your mother, she stay here."

Frank

He DIDN'T KNOW HOW HE GOT THERE, how long he'd been there, or even where he was, but he recognized Ian's face bent over him, shifting out of focus in a watery blur.

"Frank?" he heard Ian ask and wanted to answer, but before he could make his lips move, the face dissolved, and now it was back, but he couldn't move his mouth to make words. "Frank?" The voice came again, and this time he managed to groan a reply.

"Can y' hear me?" Ian asked.

Frank nodded slowly, fighting to stay above the threshold of consciousness.

"It's okay now. That ol' Finn went for a doctor."

Now Frank understood where he was, but not what had happened or how he'd got there. He knew it was bad, though. He felt his whole life slowly draining through that hole in his side.

"You'll be okay now, Frank," Ian repeated.

Frank wanted to ask what had happened, to ask where Burma was and whether she'd been hurt. He wanted to regain control of this situation, which he realized, even now, had grown too complex for Ian to handle.

"I got him for y', Frank. I killed that pimp. Now the doctor's comin'."

The pieces were starting to fall together. "Burma? Where's Burma?" he mumbled finally.

Ian shook his head—no. "She did want to come. But I told 'er nay."

The news didn't surprise him, but it didn't make him feel any better either. He thought what might happen next, knew the Finn would bring back the sheriff—not just the doctor. No one but Ian would care if Frank died, but they'd all want a piece of him before he went, a piece of Ian, too. Still, Frank knew he was too weak to travel. He'd have to let himself be taken—alive. Like this, now. Here in bed where they couldn't gun him down on the spot. Then they'd have to get him a doctor. They'd keep him in jail while he healed, maybe longer, but they'd have to let him go before long—after all, what had he done but push Fanny? Hadn't she asked for it? Hadn't he more than paid for it by getting shot? He could talk to Burma again. Then when he was strong enough to travel maybe the two of them could catch that train.

Ian stood above him, looking vacantly, silently down.

There was no way to explain this to Ian. No way to explain that he, Ian, was the one who'd done the killing, the one who had to get away, because the sheriff would be back any time and then, if there was a struggle, it would be all over. It would end right there in that room for them both. Ian had to get across the river into Wisconsin. Ruprecht wouldn't chase him too far, not for killing some pimp in a whorehouse brawl. Frank and Burma could meet him in Oregon. They'd find each other somehow. Set a place, a time . . .. Frank's mind was rushing, but his tongue was a lump of clay in the bottom of his mouth.

"You run," he finally managed, hoping Ian understood. "Oregon. River. Wisconsin. Oregon. Run. Wisconsin."

Ian's eyes—serious, determined, fighting back tears—locked hard on Frank's.

Frank wondered if he understood.

Then as if in reply, Ian shook his head—"Nay."

"Aye. Run. Wisconsin. Oregon. See you. River." The words had become a strange, groggy litany—a plea.

Ian, still looking straight into Frank's eyes, finally nodded, then bent over and embraced him, hugging hard. Then he stood up straight, and in one long motion disappeared across the room and through the hole in the floor.

"Run. Wisconsin. Oregon. River. Run." Frank continued.

Ruprecht

Fɪʀsᴛ ᴛʜᴇʀᴇ ᴡᴀs ᴛʜᴇ sʜᴏᴏᴛɪɴɢ out at Fanny's, and George's brother killed. Then, a few minutes later, with George out getting together a posse, the old Indian vomited one last time and died in the blood. Now, this crazy Finn was shouting about someone, maybe Billy's killers, up in his attic, needing a doctor.

Near as Ruprecht could tell, it was those McDonald boys that George ran out of town earlier. If so, there wasn't much the sheriff could do to save them. He knew what would happen, but he hoped to prove himself wrong.

He moved deliberately, pulling on his coat, taking the rifle from its rack, checking it, making sure, even though he knew, he had a bullet chambered. If the McDonalds were hurt as bad as the old man said, they wouldn't be going anywhere. He wanted to pick them up quietly and get them back safely in jail before George and his posse got hold of them.

First, though, Ruprecht stopped at Dr. Bonner's house, hoping to persuade the bleary-eyed physician to come by the jail and look after a sick Indian. That would serve a dual purpose: first, it would show that the Indian was alive when he left; second, it would insure the doctor was there when the wounded prisoners arrived. He might not be able to get a doctor through to the jail later, after news of the capture got around.

"Just make sure he gets plenty of rest, and I'll be by first thing in the morning to look at him," Bonner said wearily.

"Look, Doc, he won't last till mornin'," Ruprecht protested, unwilling to accept the standard late-night prescription, "and I won't have him dyin' in my jail. It's bad luck."

"If he's that sick, there won't be much I can do for him anyway."

"Look, Doc, I understand, him being just an Indian and all, but I'll see you get your full fee . . . even if I pay it myself."

"You know it isn't the money, sheriff," Bonner said with a trace of indignation.

"Sure, I know that. It's just you gotta come this time. Look, I don't ask you for much."

"Well, okay, if it's that important, I'll go."

"Good, and look Doc, wait there till I get back, will you? I might be needin' you again. There's coffee on the stove. Here. Here's the keys." Then, before Bonner could protest, Ruprecht was through the gate of the white picket fence and onto the street where the old Finn waited solemnly. The Finn was nervous, anxious to be going, and now that everything was set up, Ruprecht was, too. Holding the rifle tight to his side, he moved briskly along back to Bayshore Street and then down to Finn town.

When they reached the house, Ruprecht looked in the window but only saw the mother, sitting in a rocker sobbing into her huge handkerchief. He wanted, if possible, to take the killers without a struggle.

134

He eased open the front door, nodding the Finn to go first. The old woman, seeing her son return, jumped and ran to embrace him, wailing and crying. Ruprecht shushed her as well as he could and headed for the stairs.

He surfaced like a muskellunge through the hole in the floor. Turning his whole body in a complete circle, he raked the room with his one good eye. Only Frank was there, lying in bed, groaning almost incoherently.

"Wisconsin, Oregon, river . . .."

"Hey, ol' timer," Ruprecht yelled down the stairs, "get back up here and help me lug this fella down to jail."

Ian

H E STOOD ON A HIGH BLUFF, looking out across the ice-strewn Lake Michigan beach, barely visible in the tentative gray early morning light. A strong south wind blew across the open water, hard on his face and through his wool Mackinaw, drying the sweat that covered him like a second skin. He shivered. His chest heaved. Blood throbbing in his temples drowned out the wind-driven waves heaving ice slabs into shore, stacking them up against each other with random precision, grinding them together like gigantic teeth.

This was the first time he'd stopped running since leaving Frank. He'd worked his way back east along the route they took earlier up from the lake, after George ran them out of town.

He'd run blindly, knowing less in his mind than in his feet, where to go. Having reached the lake, however, he needed to consider. He wanted to retreat, to head back for Quebec and his family, but he remembered Frank telling about the river, about Wisconsin and Oregon. Maybe he *would* be safe once he got across the river, but to cross the river, he had to go back west through town, or somehow around it, and it would be daylight before he found the bridge and got across. Still, that's what Frank said to do. But Frank wasn't there. Ian felt dizzy again. And supposing he *did* get across the river? What then? Go on to Oregon alone? Wait there for Frank to come find him? It was impossible, beyond comprehension.

He dropped from the knoll to the icy beach, feeling whichever way he went he'd be better off along the shoreline, able to move faster than in the woods, yet not so conspicuous as on a road. But once on the beach, he grew uncertain again, began sweating again, but now with the cold, clammy sweat of terror.

The wind stiffened, and the sound of the grinding ice slabs reached him at last, echoed against the dunes and enveloped him, like the jaws of some bloodless beast devouring everything. Everything—even death. Even itself.

His chest was a knot drawn tighter and tighter. And his head began pounding again, so he jammed the heels of his hands into his eyes to press back tears that wouldn't come. Then he broke into a run, not away from the posse at all now and therefore not toward Oregon, but away from that cold grinding sound on the lake, and therefore toward home.

George

BY DAYBREAK THE HEAVY CLOUDS HAD BLOWN OFF, the wind had died, and the sun rose like a huge blood orange over the rim of the lake in the southeastern sky. But all George could see was the dogs. They were on a warm trail. And he felt good.

Not long ago, he'd come back to the jail to find Ruprecht and Dr. Bonner fussing over Frank.

"What about Billy!" George shouted. "Don't nobody care 'bout him? 'bout Billy? My brother?"

"Easy, George," Ruprecht came back. "You know we feel strong about Billy. He was one of us. Your brother. But this is different. He's gone. We gotta look after this prisoner. It's the law. We got no choice."

"No choice? We got no choice but t' nurse this bastard that killed my brother? That's the law? Then I say fuck the law. If that's the law, then fuck it! I got my own law for slime like this!"

"Gimme your keys, George," Ruprecht said flatly. But George managed to keep the keys and take half the posse on what looked like a trail leading down toward the lake. Ruprecht took the others down by the river to look for the dummy, who according to him, might be headed that way.

The two groups would put Ian in a squeeze, George pressing from behind and Ruprecht waiting ahead at the river. It was a good plan George agreed, except for one thing: it gave Ruprecht the best chance of catching the killer.

But then, after George's group arrived at the lake, the plan got confused. The dogs just milled around one spot on the beach for a while like they were lost, then headed east, not toward the river at all, and George wasn't sure if they even had a scent. Finally, he decided to follow them.

Now he knew his gamble had paid off. The dogs were hot on the trail, following into the brush from an easy, sloping curve of sandy crescents where a small creek fanned onto the beach.

Ian

H E KNEW BY THE BARKING that the posse was close. At first they'd been only an idea, something he believed might be after him, something he might have heard above the ice on the lake. But then it was dogs for sure, their eager yelping could no longer be mistaken. Still it didn't frighten him—the thought of being captured. It was almost comforting. He'd be back with Frank. He wouldn't be so alone.

And the men, the dogs? Laughable now in their frenzied pursuit, almost indistinguishable from each other. No. He wasn't afraid of them.

So now he knew it hadn't mattered which way he fled, toward Oregon or toward home, because he was meant to be caught, just like everyone will someday by someone or something they draw to themselves—magnet to magnet. Because no one escapes.

The dogs were just minutes away.

Downstream a few yards, a small trout, about the size of his hand, hung off the end of a riffle, nosing the rapid current. Ian watched for a moment, enjoyed the easy way it held place in the spring-swollen stream. He picked a small round stone from the bank and flipped it toward the trout, which darted into the shadow of some overhanging roots. Soft, early morning sunlight slanted through the trees and danced on the water.

Goodwin

H E'D BEEN LOST in a deep, dreamless sleep, and the harsh sounds that dragged him back left him slightly disoriented. Wasn't this Sunday morning? Had he overslept? And what was that noise? Dogs yelping. Men shouting and sometimes laughing. He pulled himself up slowly and made his way to the window. He pulled back the thick brown curtain. The sky was clear. He looked down his empty street toward the center of town where the noise came from, but he couldn't see its source—just the narrow, mud-slushy street and the fronts of a few stores and houses.

Not taking time to wash or shave, he threw on his clothes from last night and rushed outside. The sun was bright. The air, in spite of a slight morning chill, was light—even spring-like. He walked briskly, trying to stay on the icy patches. Rough gray, pocked with sawdust and sand, they offered better footing than the spongy ground. Then, in the shadows of the downtown buildings, the air got chilly and the ground was frozen solid. He wanted to break into a trot but thinking it unseemly, just pulled his coat tighter, tucked down his chin, clenched his shoulders, and walked faster. When he rounded a corner and emerged back into sunlight, he saw the commotion.

A crowd of about forty people, loggers and townsfolk, jostled down Bayshore. Others stared from doors and windows or milled at the mob's edge hoping to watch without getting involved. He approached one of this last group, Paul Daniels, a parishioner and owner of a dry goods store.

"Paul, what is it? They sound angry," Goodwin asked.

Daniels started, and Goodwin grew self-conscious. The shopkeeper, always fastidious, even now had his hair slicked neatly down, his moustache carefully waxed. In short, he was ready for church, as the Reverend obviously was not.

Perhaps recognition of this caused the merchant to let the hint of a smile move quickly across his face. "The other one," Daniels finally replied. "George got the other killer."

"Other killer? What other killer?" Goodwin knew nothing about even a first killer. But before Daniels could explain, the two were pressed up against the building by the crowd, which had grown steadily all through town until now it overflowed the street and flooded up onto the boardwalk where they stood.

It was a wild and unruly mob—some drinking and laughing, others angrily shouting, dogs tangled in the midst, weaving in and out yipping and barking.

Pressed against the building, Goodwin was thrown off balance. Directly behind him, a small wooden bench pressed into the back of his knees, while a logger—unshaven, smelly— pressed intentionally against his front in a hard, almost sexual way. Rolling bloodshot eyes, the logger guffawed in the Reverend's face, and Goodwin almost feinted at the stench of garlic, tobacco, and whiskey, at the sight of those rotted brown teeth. Then the man was gone, and Goodwin scrambled up onto the bench, where he could grasp the overhanging sign to keep steady against the mob.

From the height of the bench, he looked down into the crowd's center. The prisoner, a young man he'd never seen, was covered with mud, bleeding from the forehead, hands cuffed behind his back. Just above where the prisoner's hands met, George drove the rifle barrel, knocking the man face forward into the soggy street, much to the mob's delight. Some, when the prisoner went down, thrust boots through the nipping dogs to stomp him or give him a kick. Then George jerked him back to his feet and shoved him forward again.

After the crowd passed, Goodwin still gripped the sign, trying to settle himself. Slowly he loosened his grasp and climbed down. Trembling, he slumped on the bench.

"Oh my Lord," he murmured. "Heavenly Father. Has it come to this?" Yet he knew it had, just as Garrison predicted the night before. He wanted to stop the violence, but knew he was helpless. What could he say that these men would hear, and if they did hear would not mock and scorn? Nothing. He squinted up into Paul Daniels' astonished face.

"You all right, Reverend?" Daniels asked.

"Oh, yes, Paul, I believe so. Thank you," Goodwin replied. But in truth the pastor was still stunned. Slowly he regained his feet.

"Animals!" Daniels exclaimed. "Animals!" He, too, had been jostled and was straightening himself. Goodwin, standing now, glanced toward the jail, where the crowd stopped, holding the prisoner outside while George went in.

"I hope they all hang each other," Daniels added.

"I . . . I still don't understand. What's happening? Has everyone gone mad? Where's the sheriff? Please, Paul, explain this to me."

"It's those McDonald boys again," he said, "the same two that attacked Mr. Garrison. Ruprecht ran them out of town, but they snuck back out to Fanny's. First they tried to kidnap one of the girls, then killed George's brother Billy when he tried to stop them. Ruprecht got one, the big mouth, last night, and this is his brother—the one that killed Billy Kittson."

"But where's the sheriff? Where's Ruprecht? Somebody has to stop this, to restore order."

"I don't know where Ruprecht is. Inside the jail, I guess."

Even before the answer came, Goodwin realized Robert had been right about the sheriff. Only one person in Menominee could take control now and reestablish order, not a man of the cloth, not a man of the law, only Robert Garrison.

"Excuse me, Paul," Goodwin said. "I must go for help."

Ruth

S HE TOLD THE CHILDREN TO DRESS FOR CHURCH, but they wouldn't be distracted from Reverend Goodwin, who stood in the foyer, disheveled, unshaven, panting through his open mouth. They knew it wasn't time for church. And they had heard the sounds of commotion coming from town.

"Where's . . . where's Robert? Please, children, quickly go find your father," Goodwin gasped, sending Mary and Bobby off toward Robert's study.

Ruth sought the cause of the trouble, but Goodwin said only that she needn't worry, there was no immediate danger, it would all work out in the end. Then Robert arrived and sent the children upstairs and Ruth to the kitchen, where she stood, ear to the door. She sensed that this was related to the trouble of the past two nights, but not how. Then, hearing Robert approach across the dining room floor, she busied herself at the stove.

"Don't be upset, Ruth," Robert said. "There's been a killing, and the murderers have been captured, but the sheriff has lost control, and Reverend Goodwin believes I can restore order. He and I are going down to the jail together to do what we can."

Ruth gasped slightly, but audibly. She knew Robert was more deeply involved than he let on, but not how, yet she couldn't ask directly.

"But Robert," she probed, "how should this be our concern? These murderers? Cutthroats? That disgusting sheriff? Please. Don't get your family involved with that sort of thing. Think of us. Think of your children."

"I am thinking of you. That's why I must go. Those two men, the killers, Reverend Goodwin thinks they might be the same two who attacked me last night. They've returned and killed one of our people. The sheriff has lost control. A mob is on the streets, drunk, destroying property. One drunken logger even threatened the Reverend, just moments ago. We have to stop them—or who knows where they might turn. No, Ruth. We have to stand up for this town—for our family, everything we believe in."

"Do be careful," she finally said, touching her hand to his coat sleeve. He stood firm and unbending, almost a tree. Then, slowly he lifted his arm, brushing her back. He patted her cheek.

"Don't worry. Reverend Goodwin stands with me," Robert said. Then, hurriedly, he headed back through the dining room to the foyer, where the minister waited, muddy and distraught, fidgeting nervously. "Just stay inside and keep the doors locked," Robert said, turning toward her. Although he looked straight into her face, and she into his, their eyes never met.

"Good bye, Ruth," Goodwin stammered as her husband ushered him out the door.

"Aren't you two dressed for church yet?" Ruth scolded at

the children, who had been watching unnoticed from the landing halfway down the stairs.

"Where did they go?" Mary asked.

"Just into town to take care of some business."

"On Sunday? Before church? With the Reverend?" Clearly Mary knew she was being lied to, but right now, Ruth didn't care.

"Yes," she insisted. "That's right. Now you two get upstairs this instant and dress for church. Your father will want to leave the minute he returns, and Lord help us all if you're not ready."

"But . . . ," Bobby started to object.

"No 'buts' about it. Upstairs, the both of you this instant." And then she was alone, back in the kitchen looking at the stove, wondering what she was after. She picked up a dishtowel and wiped a small swirl of milk from the oilcloth table cover.

It could have been any Sunday morning, but it wasn't. Something dark and ugly curled around the edges of her life. She didn't know what, but she knew Robert did, and Reverend Goodwin, too. And she knew it all began on Friday and had grown more tangled and sinister ever since. She knew it involved not just those two loggers, but another woman, too. And now, right now, as she folded the dishtowel and hung it back on the rack, Reverend Goodwin and her husband were out there again, getting themselves, getting her too, her and the children and everyone, even the pastor himself, more deeply involved with murder, with drunkenness, adultery, and other vile, barely imaginable sins.

Except for Samson's soft, thin singing in the parlor, the house was quiet. And how, Ruth wondered, sighing, could any good possibly come of this half-frozen, half-ravaged country? She wished Robert, or even the pastor was there so she could ask him the question. But they were gone. She was alone again, as she was almost every day—with the children and her thoughts.

Robert

G ARRISON WOULDN'T YIELD TO RUPRECHT, who had tried to dominate with a glassy stare and a slow, confident voice. Now Robert leaned into the sheriff's face, backing him up. The two stood in front of the large desk. Only Ruprecht's rifle, held crosswise over his chest, separated them. Except for Frank, who lay unconscious, and his cellmate, the dead Indian, the two were alone.

Goodwin, who had hung back a safe distance from the mob, didn't follow Robert up onto the porch, where George now stood above Ian, his personal hostage, beating his rifle butt on the jailhouse door.

"You wait here," Robert had said, when he felt Goodwin's pace slowing. He didn't want to coax and explain. He wanted to act first and explain later. "I'll be right back. Stay put," he said. "All right!" he shouted at the men, many of whom worked under him, "Step aside now! I'm coming through! See here now! Move! Move!" And the mob parted then closed behind him again as he burst onto the porch.

He looked first at George and then down at the limp, bloody prisoner. Yes, it was the same man, McDougall, the big one who wouldn't talk.

150

"Is Ruprecht in there?" he asked instead, pointing to the door.

"Yeah, but he won't let anyone in but this bastard." George pointed to Ian. "And I ain't givin' him up."

"Ruprecht, this is Garrison!" Robert pounded the door. "Let me in!" The door cracked, just a small dark slit with a barrel sticking out.

"Okay," the sheriff said softly, opening it further with his left hand, aiming the rifle at Garrison's gut with his right.

Robert entered slowly, looking around.

"Close that door and bolt it," Ruprecht ordered.

Garrison eyed him a moment without moving, then let the door swing shut.

"Bolt it!" Ruprecht repeated.

"What are you afraid of, Sheriff? Your own deputy?"

"Shut up and bolt that damned door."

"I will warn you now. Set that gun down."

"Not till you bolt the door."

Garrison bolted the door.

"Sorry to treat you like this, Mr. Garrison." Ruprecht lowered the rifle. "But I gotta do my job. I got a prisoner to protect."

"Protect him!? You wave a gun in my face to protect him? Is that right? And what about that mob out there? Reverend Goodwin has been assaulted. There's no telling who might be next—our wives, our children. No telling who those roughnecks might turn on if you don't control them."

"I'm only one man. I got my hands full right here."

"Then you won't even talk to them?"

151

"You can't talk sense to a mob like that. Wouldn't do no good. You just gotta wait 'em out, hope they get tired and go home." Ruprecht's glass eye drifted off to the side.

"I think you're afraid," Garrison challenged.

"Listen, mister," the sheriff shot back, "I'm not afraid of you. You better know that right now, and I'm not afraid of them either. But I'm not a fool. No way in hell anyone's gonna break that mob up before they're ready. There's two choices: wait 'em out or give 'em what they want, and I'm waitin'."

Garrison weighed the alternatives. "Well, you might have to try something else," he finally said.

"Get outta here, mister," Ruprecht snapped. "We got nothing to talk about."

Garrison felt his blood rising. He was accustomed to giving, not taking orders. With a long, unblinking stare, he surveyed the sheriff: red hair, straight and strawlike, stuck out of his misshapen head; a few more hairs hung from his blue-veined nose. A gold incisor gleamed in his half open mouth. "I'll have your neck for this," Garrison sputtered, but his voice had lost its conviction, and the words sounded weak, almost pathetic.

"Not *my* neck I'm worried about right now," Ruprecht replied. Then, with his rifle, he motioned toward the door.

Robert unbolted it and stepped outside.

"What's up?" George asked as the door slammed shut and the bolt fell back into place.

"The sheriff has taken leave of his senses. That's all."

"That ain't news," George replied.

"We've got to break up this mob. Right now. Before it gets out of control."

"Outta control?" the deputy laughed. "Hell, I been with this bunch from the start 'n they never been *in* control!"

"Well, we have to stop them! Break them up before they turn on the town, our families, our businesses!"

Some of the more daring had already begun breaking into saloons and dragging liquor out into the streets. Soon they'd start after money. After that there'd be no stopping them. They could turn the town inside out—and then just disappear into the woods. Robert imagined them entering his home, ransacking it, cornering Ruth. Or breaking into his office, forcing him to open the safe, setting fire to the mill.

"You get that other swamp rat out here and we'll take care of everything. We'll string 'em both up fast and it'll be all over."

"No," Garrison replied. "Not that. I don't condone violence."

"That ain't what Billy said."

"What? What did Billy tell you."

"He said you was a real bear out there 't Fanny's. Ain't that right?" George chuckled slightly.

Robert had no reply. He turned and faced the crowd—a familiar bunch, always ready for violence and destruction—loggers, drunkards, gamblers, bar girls, a few of his mill hands and Indians, too. Ruth was right: none of this was properly his concern. There was no reason to involve himself with their ilk, to subject himself to this abuse. His responsibilities were to his family and business. What did he care about these creatures—the whores, the cardsharps, the loggers, any of them—as long as they didn't interfere with business and kept in their own part of town? He touched his still-swollen nose. Hadn't he taken enough? He turned back to George.

153

"I won't lead a lynch mob, if that's what you're thinking."

"They don't need t' be led. You just knock on that door 'n tell Ruprecht you wanna come in again. I'll take care of the rest."

Robert briefly considered George's offer, looked back at the mob, then pounded the door with his fist.

Ruprecht

JUST AS THE SHERIFF UNDID THE LATCH, George pushed Robert inside, and the two of them, Garrison and Ruprecht, tumbled back onto the floor. During the melee, George dragged Ian inside and re-bolted the door. As the deputy stood over the heap, Garrison struggled to his feet.

"Araggah! My back!" Ruprecht complained. "Where's that damn gun? You bastards can't . . . Arraraggah . . . My back!"

"Get clear, Mr. Garrison," George shouted, pulling Robert to his feet. "He's old, but he's fast—fast 'n sneaky. Here." George held the keys out for Robert. "Open that cell. We'll keep him there till it's over."

But Garrison wouldn't take the keys.

"Come on, Mr. Garrison," George insisted. "I got a gun on him. Least you can do is open the door." Garrison still didn't move. "That's the last thing," George went on. "That's all y' gotta do."

Garrison still balked, but when George tossed the keys, he caught them, and stiffly, hesitantly, opened the cell. Shoulders hunched forward, he fumbled the key. Though neither it nor the hole was too small, he had trouble getting it in. Then it was hard to turn.

Ruprecht wanted to laugh, not at Garrison's awkwardness, but at being locked up—safe in his own cell, out of harm's way. Yes, at Garrison, too, for while he was powerful and in some ways shrewd, he was clumsy with fear and anger. Those two forces pulled him in opposite directions, made him awkward, kept him off-balance—like here: no one, not even George, hated those McDonald boys more than Garrison, but the superintendent was afraid to get involved. Jump forward while you jerk back, that's his way, Ruprecht thought.

"C'mon, ol' man," George said, prodding Ruprecht with the rifle.

"Watch that gun, you fool!" the sheriff snapped back. "Can't you see my back went out. Oh, Jeeesus!" He crawled, almost slithered into the cell.

George had already dragged Frank out, but the Indian was still there, stiffening in the corner. George took the key from Garrison, slammed the door, and locked it.

"Hey! Get this ol' chief outta here!" Ruprecht called. "He's startin' to stink."

George

"WHOOHEEE! WE DID IT. We Goddamn *did* it!" George laughed, slapping the big ring of keys on the desk. "I just wish Billy could'a been here, that's all." He glanced over at Garrison, who stood near the cell door.

Garrison's face revealed nothing.

"Fanny told me *you* did *this* to Billy," George said, grinding and twisting a boot into Frank's blood-soaked side. "But Billy's not here. He's dead." George kicked hard into Frank's side again. "Billy's dead 'n you swamp rats done it." He kicked him again. "Well, I'm gonna kill you, too, Goddamn it. You gonna be dead, too, y' hear?"

Frank didn't answer.

George kicked him again. He felt the excited mob outside. "C'mon," he yelled at Robert. "Let's do it now! Let's string the bastards up!"

"Stop it, you fool," Garrison snapped. "This isn't a party. This is serious business. It must be handled properly."

George was brought up short. He thought Garrison's part was over, that he'd already gone farther than he wanted to and would just hang back in the shadows till it was done. He didn't like Robert stepping forward to wrestle control back, to make him a lackey.

"Now just wait a minute," he shot back, but while he searched for more words, Garrison broke in.

"You do as I say, and you'll be sheriff when this is done. I'll see to that." His voice was tense and controlled now like the string of a tightly drawn bow.

Feeling the tension, George knew Garrison had been holding his bow at full bent a long time—too long. George knew the feeling, how your fingers begin to tremble, then your forearm, your upper arm and shoulder, till your eyes start to glaze and it gets hard to stay locked on target so that finally you have to lower the bow slowly and release tension, or just let fly and hope for the best. George saw that was Garrison's choice right now. And he saw that Robert could no longer lower the bow, without getting off his shot. He'd committed too much of himself, knocking on the jailhouse door, locking Ruprecht up. Outside, the whole town was watching, waiting to see what he'd do next. And so, for the first time, George was certain, really certain, that Garrison could be trusted to bring it off.

"Okay," George said. "I got it. You just say what to do."

"That's right. You've got it. Everything is under control." Robert straightened up. Watching George steadily, he walked to the desk, took the key ring, then said, "First we must bring that crowd under control. They're dangerous. Then I want you to get me Culhane and Reverend Goodwin."

Now George was puzzled again. It looked to him like the mob was just ripping to go. Why quiet them down? He should be getting a strong rope now and a preacher when it was done. But then, George had made Garrison boss, so he knew he had no choice but to follow orders.

"Go out now," Garrison said. "Quiet that crowd. I've got to think. And here. Here, take *them*." He pointed at Frank and Ian. "I don't want to be left alone with them. Take them both outside and guard them."

George picked his rifle up from the desk and walked over to Frank, who lay curled in a half-fetal position, grabbed him by the collar, and dragged him outside. Ian, who could still walk, staggered ahead.

As George opened the door, he saw the crowd had swollen to about twice its original size. The number of townspeople remained about the same, a tight angry cluster near the porch. Because their anger was vague and undirected, they became a kind of buffer between the jail and the restless loggers, who hung around the edges and whose numbers even now were growing. Occasionally, from out on the periphery, someone tossed an empty whiskey bottle or a threat—"String them bastards up by the balls!"—over the townspeople onto the wooden porch.

Ian, hunched with his back against the wall and his head tucked between upraised knees, looked like he was trying to shut everything out. What most enraged George was that he wouldn't even admit what he'd done, wouldn't deny it either, just stared in your face with a blank look that wasn't rage or fear or anything a normal man might feel. Dumbness, just plain empty dumbness, and that dummy killed Billy.

George wanted to hurt him. Hurt him bad.

He dumped Frank on top of him, and for just a second, feeling the limp weight, thought Frank might have been dead. But no, he was still twitching some.

159

"All right!" George shouted, raising his rifle above his head, trying to get the crowd's attention. But no one paid him any mind, so he squeezed the trigger and sent a shot ripping off into the sky. Now it was silent—every eye fixed on him. "All right!" he yelled again. "This ain't a Goddamn party! This is serious business. This ain't a game!"

"Come on, lawman!" someone shouted.

"String 'em up now!" chimed in another.

"They give us *all* a bad name!" screamed a third.

"Killers! Murderers!" shouted someone else.

George cracked another shot into the air. They fell silent again.

"Hold on," he called out. "I'm in charge here, 'n I'm gonna see this done right! String 'em up? Sure," he said, his voice almost breaking, "they gonna pay for what they done. They killed my brother. We gonna see to that. But we gotta do it right. That's the law! Now where's Goodwin? Garrison wants Reverend Goodwin inside. Somebody get him up here so we can get goin'.'"

"Reverend?" someone yelled. "What the hell we gonna do? Have a sermon?"

"Onwarrrd Chrischunn Sooldjurrs!" an inebriated voice proclaimed and then began singing in a low, rolling, drunken rhythm. The townspeople turned and tried to shout him into submission, but still he went on, staggering forward now, bottle in hand. A few others fell in behind him in a column of mock Salvationists, all singing—"with the crosh of Jeeshus, flowing on before." George was about to fire the gun again, but he saw the Reverend, white and trembling, being pulled up through the crowd.

"This, this is an outrage! An abomination," Goodwin gasped as he stumbled onto the porch. Recovering his balance, he studied the prisoners briefly and shrunk back. "This is Satan's work, all his work. And on the Lord's day. On the Sabbath. On Sunday."

George almost laughed at Goodwin, wailing and raving like an old woman over a hurt cat, but when their eyes met, he saw pain, confusion, and fear, so he choked the laugh back down.

"Thanks for comin', Reverend," he said in his best, starched Sunday school voice. "Mr. Garrison's inside waitin' on you. I hope you two figure somethin' out fast. I don't know how long I can hold this mob off."

Goodwin hurried past into the jail.

"Damn," George muttered and looked out over the crowd. The Salvationist parade had turned into a wrestling match. A few loggers ran up to the cheering mob, their arms full of looted whiskey. "Damn, I sure would like to be out there havin' some a' that fun." But, such was the price of responsibility, George knew he had a more important role to play. He squeezed the trigger and the rifle cracked again. "All right!" he shouted. "Settle down! This ain't no party!"

"Come on, law! Let's take him now!" a voice shouted, and as George felt the crowd tightening around him, he turned and stuck his head in the door.

"This is it, Mr. Garrison," he called. "I can't hold 'em back no more." He waved the rifle high above his head. "Heeeyahhee! Come on! Let's go! Let's take 'em! Let's do it!"

Ian

W HEN THEY DUMPED FRANK ON HIM, he knew it but couldn't
move, and so now when the deputy lifted Frank off him
and jerked him to his feet, he understood what was coming,
and he wasn't alarmed or anxious. He just didn't care. He was
already numb—inside and out.

"All right, you sorry bastard, this is it," the deputy snarled
and shoved Frank in Ian's face. "I can't stand to touch this
filthy bastard. You take him."

So, Ian, though he could barely walk, took Frank again.
Buffeted by the crowd, he had little control of his movements. The deputy prodded him forward till he thought he'd
fall, but the crowd propped him up, so he kept on his feet.
And then Frank was so heavy, so limp and cold, and Ian's fingers grew weaker and he didn't think he could hang on anymore when something sharp and hard crashed into his forehead and he felt something warm and wet run down over
one eye and into his mouth, which was open and gasping.
And all around he heard the mob laughing and cursing him,
close-up yet distant, and it was all so far beyond even pain
or rage that he was on the verge of laughter, too, and then he
went down.

They were fighting about him—no, fighting about what to do next.

And he saw someone drag Frank to a nearby wrought iron gate and spear him like a fish on the sharp black spikes. Then it was a tangle of legs and faces again, and he understood they'd do the same thing to *him* on a neighboring gate. He felt them lifting him.

"There!" he heard someone say just before it went black, "That'll hold 'em till the rope gets here!"

Garrison

ROBERT WATCHED FROM THE PORCH STEP—the greater part of him horrified and revolted, but another, smaller part intrigued, even attracted to the drama, these two shanty boys who attacked him the day before, speared on iron gates. One looked dead but the other was writhing, flailing.

The mob was waiting for rope. Idiots, he thought. Idiots. Halfway into it before they think of rope!

He'd sent Goodwin back to be with Ruth and the children: to explain why he was needed downtown and to tell them everything was under control. And in a way everything was under control, for despite all the violence, the clumsy mistakes, this could hardly have gone better. Garrison knew that he, himself, couldn't be held responsible. It was George who turned the mob loose, not him. He'd been inside consulting Goodwin about the morality of the lynching and whether Goodwin would give it his sanction.

A roar went up from the crowd as they saw the rope coming.

"Gimme that!" George hollered, grabbing it from a logger. "It's my brother they killed. Now I'm gettin' even." He cut the rope with his buck knife and tied off two quick nooses. He noosed Ian first, then Frank.

164

The crowd laughed at something George did, but Robert stood too far back to see what. He moved in closer, but not so close he might get caught up in the act. Now, pulling on the rope, George lifted the two from their gates.

An old, moon-faced woman came forward, spit in Frank's face, and cursed him in words Robert couldn't quite understand. Robert was about to move in closer, but the crowd grabbed the ropes, as in tug o' war and dragged the killers away.

Maybe because Ian and Frank looked like dogsleds gliding down mudslick ruts in the sawdust road, or maybe because the air was sunny-chill and light with the first blush of spring, or maybe for some other reason, people—at first only children, later grown-ups as well—began riding the criminals as the crowd dragged them along.

Garrison almost left then, almost went home to Ruth and the Reverend, but he knew he might be called on later to testify, and so felt obliged to observe.

"Get the hell offa there!" George shouted at a heavy man who tried to catch a ride on Frank. "You wanna pull his head off? Then how we gonna hang him?"

The fat man gestured obscenely at George and jumped with both feet on the corpse. Blood squirted from the hole in Frank's side. The procession stopped.

"What's a matter with you?" George shouted. "Can't you hear?"

"Aw hell," the man replied. "I gotta have my fun, too. Besides, he can't feel it. He's already dead, ain't he?"

"How should I know? I'm no doctor. All I know is we ain't

hung him yet, and his head's about t' pop. How we gonna hang a man without a head?"

"String him up by the balls!" someone shouted, and the processional resumed. Looking for a serviceable tree, they headed down Bayshore, past Beech Street toward the far end of town, where a few gnarly hardwoods still stood uncut. But that was over a mile, and the bodies were pretty torn up by now. The riding slowed things too much, so the mob settled for kicking and stepping on the prisoners, sometimes with caulked boots, digging with sharp-pointed spikes. Almost everyone got in a few good stomps. The reluctant who tried to hang back and watch were persuaded, even pushed, to the front and pressed to join in—Culhane, Maki, LaChance, Daniels—all of them, loggers and townspeople alike. All except Garrison, who followed at a measured distance. No one dared force him, though it might have been possible.

"Hold up here," George said and raised the rifle high. They were at the railroad crossing. George pointed out a big sign on a thick pine post. "LOOK OUT FOR THE CARS" it said in crude, hand-drawn black letters. "This is good enough. These two don't need a tree. We better hang 'em here while we still got something to hang." He threw Frank's rope up over the sign. "Here, Pikey," he said, tossing the other rope end to a friend. "You take that one. We can haul 'em up together."

Pikey threw his rope up, and they both pulled at once, but it wasn't easy. Finally, after some strenuous tugging and jerking, George and Pikey got the two limp bodies up so their feet were off the ground and lashed the ropes to the post.

It should have been a moment of celebration and triumph,

but it wasn't. At the sight of those blood-soaked, mud-covered corpses twisting slowly in the late-morning sun, the crowd fell silent.

Robert had to turn away. Others, strong men, men accustomed to human blood, unmoved by the taking of life, did too. A chubby, peach-faced kid near the front of the crowd vomited on the man in front of him, a logger, who spun and clobbered the kid with his forearm.

A woman sobbed.

"Get them down!" Robert shouted. "Cut them down now!" But nobody moved. He ran to George and grabbed his arm. "Get them down. We can't leave them here in the middle of town. We must get them down!"

"I don't know," George mused, "I kinda like 'em there. Just hangin' there to show what happens when you mess with a Kittson."

"Our wives will see them. Our children. No. They must come down now. Look, they're in the way of the sign. They'll scare the horses, cause an accident. No. They must come down now."

Daniels and some others who'd been listening agreed.

"Well, where do we take 'em? What do we do?"

"Get them in the ground fast!"

"Bury 'em?" George asked. The earth was too frozen for that.

"Bury 'em, hell," someone shouted. "Take 'em out to Fanny's!" George's eyes met Pikey's. Quickly, they undid the ropes and let the bodies fall. Then they were off. No one rode this time. They were all running now. The bodies, heads somehow still intact, trailed behind at the end of their tethers.

Garrison, relieved to see the crowd headed out of town, trotted along, off by himself to the side. Things could get out of hand any moment.

Burma

S HE HEARD THEM BEFORE SHE SAW THEM, before they even
reached the clearing, where the path came out of the jack
pines. And then she saw them—the mob streamed out of the
trees, tramping the curled brown ferns and the small twisty
sumac. They were dragging something on a rope, but the window was dirty and she couldn't see what. They looked victori-
ous, almost festive, drinking and laughing as they came,
though it was still late morning.

And then the first of them reached the porch, and she
could see into the crowd, and she realized what it was—who
it was—they were dragging. She recoiled from the window.

But by then they were on the stairs. She heard their heavy
boots and Fanny's hollering, and she knew who they wanted.
She drew her kimono up tight. She bolted the door, threw herself against it.

But they smashed it, splintered it, and she fell back on the
floor and someone shouted, "There she is! We got her now!"

And someone else yanked her by the hair to her feet.

Another grabbed her wrists and pinched her hands tight
together behind her.

Then a thick, muscular hand tore open her kimono.

She looked into the face of the man attached to that hand. It was George Kittson.

"Whore! Goddamn whore! It's your fault! I told Billy, 'Leave her be, she's just a whore,' but Billy wouldn't listen. Thought he was in love. Fucking bitch!" He smashed her face with his wrist and the back of his hand. Then he snorted up a mouthful of tobacco juice and mucous and spit it out onto her chest. It ran slowly between her breasts. The men followed with their eyes as it traced the curve of her tummy and settled in the small puff of hair where her legs met.

Somebody snickered.

"Shut up!" George snapped. "Get her on the bed! Get loverboy in here."

She saw them drag in Ian's ravaged body.

"Not him, Goddammit! You got the wrong one! That's the one killed Billy. His brother's the ladies' man. Get *him* in here!" So they kicked Ian aside and dragged in Frank. "Somebody take his clothes off!" George ordered, but nobody moved to do it. So he pushed Burma down on the bed and lifted the bloody hulk, wet-cold and lifeless, still fully clothed. As he dumped it on her, the men cheered.

And finally, as George began pushing the corpse up and down on top of her in furious mock intercourse, she started to scream. George's eyes burned into hers. "Get Garrison in here. Get him in and give *him* his turn! I hear *he* likes her, too!"

The crowd roared approval, and a second later she saw Robert, the same man who'd hurt her on Friday, being pushed through the crowd, his face white and frightened above her.

170

He struggled, trying to escape, shouting something that went unheard over the noise.

George pushed him down on the corpse.

And then it began all over, not just the corpse this time, but Garrison too, Frank between them like meat in a sandwich, and on top pushing—not just George anymore but four or five men all together, yelling madly above the sound of the plunging bedsprings, and Garrison shouting, too, and Burma, her voice winding out and around all the others and blending with them into a single mad crescendo of ecstatic despair, until all that remained in that room was the violent pulsating rhythm of that cry of insane release.

And then it was over. As suddenly as they appeared, they were gone.

She lay there alone on the bed, shaken and bruised and bloody—but still alive. She shivered a little, looking around to make sure no one had hung back behind to hurt her again. She heard them downstairs arguing, and then she heard glass breaking, people running, slamming doors.

"Fire!" they called. "Get out! Fire!"

She pulled herself up and stumbled to the door, where she looked down the long staircase and saw part of the living room filled with smoke. She tightened her kimono again, grabbed up her still-packed carpet bag, and stumbled down. The way to the front door was blocked with flames, so she fled through the kitchen, out the back door to where Fanny and the girls were huddled, maybe fifty yards from the house, surrounded by yelping dogs, held by short ropes in a circle. Fanny stood with her left foot up on a metal cash box, holding the revolver.

Across the clearing, Burma saw the crowd watching the fire, while the two McDonald boys hung limp and wasted from a single scraggly pine.

The McDonald Boys, Menominee, Michigan.

Goodwin

H<small>E SAT IN A WARM SHAFT OF SUNLIGHT</small> that fell on the Garrison's velour sofa. Samson hopped in his cage from perch to perch. The children were upstairs keeping quiet. Ruth was in the kitchen doing something—not crying, he hoped. It was hot there in the parlor, with the sun soaking into his black wool coat, and he perspired slightly. He still hadn't shaved or brushed his hair, although it was now almost noon, long past time for the morning service, for his undelivered sermon. He felt dirty and stale and useless. He wanted to go home and wash up. He wondered what Robert and the men were doing, whether he should arrange a service for later that afternoon.

And yet, for all he wanted to leave, he knew he should stay with Ruth until Robert returned and told them the lynching, or whatever it was, was over.

Ruth had been so upset, so confused and worried, he was afraid she might break down completely if he left her. He wished he could comfort her, touch her—not with his hand, that was too much even to think of—but a word or a look. She only wanted one thing, though—information about Robert. And the Reverend, though it hurt to withhold it, would not give it.

"I can only say this, Ruth," he said. "Robert is a good man and a strong man. Many others rely on him. He carries a heavy weight of responsibility. Like any man in his position, he is sometimes pushed to his limits, but he has the power of the Lord in his heart. He is a fortress of hope in times of adversity. We must be strong and keep him strong. We must give him our trust, our support."

Ruth's back was to him, and he could tell from the way her shoulders trembled ever so slightly, from the way her small hands went up to her face, that she was crying.

"We must all bear our crosses as best we can," he said. "We must remain firm in our faith, whatever comes."

She turned and looked at him wordlessly, her eyes moist and swollen, her nose a little red. Her chin trembled slightly.

"Don't cry, Ruth," he said. "Robert will be home soon, and he will explain it all. All will be well again soon. The Lord is a perfect master, Ruth . . ."

But she turned sharply away and hurried into the kitchen, where she had remained ever since.

Ruprecht

T HE SHERIFF SHIVERED as he sat on the small, wooden bunk thrust against the cell door. He wedged his nose and part of his cheeks out between the bars, hoping for air.

The Indian had begun to smell pretty bad. Though the window had been left open, that didn't help. It just let the cold in, or seemed to, without letting the stench out. The stove had long since burnt out and cooled, and the jail too had cooled almost to the outside temperature. So he wrapped himself in a coarse wool blanket and went and hung his nose out toward the window. He was waiting for George or somebody else to come let him out.

He wanted to hear what had happened. He wanted to confront, to accuse, to punish, to forgive.

George would be easiest to handle. His punishment would be to bury the loggers, make a cross to put over each grave, bury his brother's killers. But not now. This was a bad time to bury the dead. The ground was still frozen in its depths. You had to bury too shallow this time of year, and then dogs or even wolves would come dig up the grave. No, he'd make George wait and do it right. He'd watch and make sure it was done right. Bury not just the loggers, but the Indian too, and all the rest out there in the gravedigger's shack, stacked up all winter in their white pine coffins waiting for thaw.

The coffins kept in some odor, but not all, and this time of year, between when the frozen bodies thawed and the earth was ready to receive them, that shack could smell pretty bad, even worse than the jail right now. So that would take care of George. It would even the score, remind him where he stood.

Garrison would be harder. Of course, the courts couldn't touch him, wouldn't want to anyway, Ruprecht knew that. There'd be an inquiry, but nothing would come of it. Everyone would have a different story, claiming innocence and forcing the blame somewhere else until nobody even remembered it right anymore, and didn't know whether to believe their own story or somebody else's or whether it was real or all just a dream, like swamp gas—a will-o'-the-wisp. That's the way these things go, Ruprecht thought. He'd seen it happen before. It was always the same.

I'll make Garrison pay slowly, he thought. I'll make him pay a little every time he comes near me, on the streets, in his office, everywhere. So everyone will know, not just him. And I'll stop when I'm ready, not before.

The thought felt good. As for missing the lynching, he didn't mind. He was too old for that sort of fun. He knew it was bad for his heart.

Garrison

MONDAY MORNING ROBERT ROSE EARLY and left the house quietly, the children sleeping, Ruth pretending sleep. As he stepped into the predawn darkness, the streets were empty, and he was glad to reach the mill unobserved. Like the house, it was silent. He wanted to hear saws again, the low, busy hum of people at work, of life back to normal again.

He tried to work, himself, but couldn't. His mind kept flashing from one moment to another, reliving the weekend's events. He tried to focus his thoughts, control them, but they kept slipping and twisting, turning inside out.

On Sunday he'd closed the topic with Ruth and Goodwin. All three had come to an unspoken understanding that the incident, like a bad dream, should never be mentioned among them, that no good could come of pursuing it, that it would only cause hurt, more pain to all, that they all had suffered enough. A time to forgive, they had agreed. A time to pray.

He walked to the window. A half-loaded schooner was docked in the harbor. Her bare masts swayed slightly in rhythm with the breeze and the water. Fresh cut lumber lay out on the pier, waiting to be loaded for Chicago. The docks stood deserted. The booming grounds, too, remained empty of men.

Robert walked into the large, open room by the mill's front door. He looked out a dirty window and down the long street. It was light out by now, but no one had shown up for work.

"Where are they? Where are the men?" he muttered half aloud, pulling out his watch. He had deadlines and quotas to meet. It was getting late.

Burma

T HE WELT ON HER CHEEK where George had smacked her still ached and tingled when she touched it. The bruise ran black and swollen from above her left eye to her lip, so she had trouble breathing on that side. She had trouble standing long, too. So she sat leaning over the small, round table, dark hair fanned out veil-like over half her face, full carpetbag by her foot. She had taken quite a pounding over the past few days.

Fanny and the girls had been put up at the Montreal House by Henri Picard, till "arrangements" were made. But Burma had no arrangements to make.

She ached everywhere, not just from her fitful night's sleep, head down on a table, but from days of being slapped and shoved and yelled at, waves of hatred, revulsion and love. Yes, that too—and even, however briefly, hope. For where love is, there hope is found. But now as though set in a cast, she sat fixed in the same cramped position she'd slept in most of the night, leaning forward, right cheek on the back of her hands, which served as a pillow, left cheek turned upward, her eye-slit only a squint beneath her loose hair.

Across the table, Lily sat studying her nails, ears attuned

to the conversation at the bar, where Fanny and Picard stood close together.

"They're gonna send us all over to Escanaba till things settle down," she said.

"Not me," Burma said. "I've had enough. I'm not takin' it anymore." She lifted her head and looked away from the bar, past the tables and the new chandelier to a slant of morning sunlight from the open front door. "Not much of a choice we got, Lily," she said. "Guess you could almost say no choice at all. What they think. What they want us to think. No choice but to buckle back under. Take some more morphine. Go where they tell us. Do what they say."

"That's how it is for someone like us. Couple a whores like us. What else can we do? Just let it be, girl. This'll all heal over. Like everything else. We'll be okay."

"Then you'd best go to Escanaba if that's how you think," Burma replied. "I can't see it like that anymore. Not after all this that's happened. I've felt and seen too much these past few days." She nodded toward the carpetbag. "When I packed up and came downstairs two days ago, I made up my mind. Whatever happened, whatever Fanny did, whatever anyone did, I'm moving on. I'm going to Oregon. And that hasn't changed." She grasped the bag and pushed back her chair. She rose deliberately, if somewhat unsteadily, to her feet. "He's dead now. He didn't make it. But we can. We can still catch that train out of here." With her left hand, she brushed back the hair from over her eyes and stepped off toward the light slanting in from the doorway. As she took her second step, she heard Lily's chair scrape back across the coarse wooden floor.

"Well, let's go then," Lily said. "We got a long journey ahead."

Made in the USA